an

AWFULLY
BIG
ADVENTURE

A NEW SEQUEL TO

PETER
PAN

GEORGE R MITCHELL

Cover design by Angelina Antiukova

Typesetting by Raspberry Creative Type, Edinburgh

To my dad . . .

I'm eternally grateful for being able
to read this book to you before you passed.
Thank you for your inspiration, support
and constant belief in me.

'When you wish upon a star . . .'

Part One

CHAPTER 1

'Is there no escape from this wretched sun? Smee? Smee? Mr Smee!' The hot empty beach echoed to the irritable bellow. 'Where the devil are you?' Then, more quietly and to himself, 'Now, where's my hat?'

The old man needed his hat more than ever these days. With his black, curly hair long gone, his bare head burned within minutes.

Not that his famous flowing black curls were ever real – he'd been bald for years. But no one knew he wore a wig, apart from his second in command, his loyal servant, Mr Smee. It was the best-kept secret in Neverland. Or one of them, anyway.

And who is this pitiful, bald, complaining old man? Of course, it's Captain Hook, the pirate once feared above all others. Can you see him in your mind's eye right now? Standing tall and commanding with his hook gleaming, immaculately dressed, his captain's hat at just the right angle, and that long black hair flowing down around his face and proud moustache. Confident, scary, powerful.

But it was always a sham.

And now, with his glorious captain a shadow of his former self, Smee was worried. After nearly being eaten alive by that crocodile, Hook had been stranded on this tiny uninhabited island in the middle of the ocean for almost a year, with only Smee for company. Captain James Hook was, without a doubt, a broken man.

Smee had long known Hook wore a wig, along with the special shoes with secret insteps to make him look taller. And the false teeth. Oh, the thought of those teeth made him shudder – it had been Smee's job to remove them from Hook's mouth every evening and put them in a glass of water by his bed. He even knew that, for many years, Hook had secretly worn a lady's corset to hold in his ever-growing belly.

But once he'd got the boss fully kitted-out every morning and he walked out onto the deck of the *Jolly Roger*, there stood a man to be feared. Captain James Hook. The greatest pirate who ever lived.

Now? The captain's teeth had been lost at sea and his old corset long ago transformed into a sunshade to protect his head. And the famous wig? Its whereabouts were unknown.

Carrying an armful of assorted fruits, Mr Smee walked back along the hot, sandy beach towards their little hut, taking in the sight ahead of him. Sitting on a rock, a bald, short, toothless man. His saggy belly hanging out over dirty, torn trousers. His hook? Not worn for months. It lay, seemingly unwanted, in the corner of their makeshift beach hut.

Smee himself was unremarkable to look at. Medium height and medium build, he had no defining features. His only trademark was a purple bandana, which he wore either around his neck or on his head. But he was a joyful soul.

Smee walked over to his captain and handed him a large, ripe lemon, which he'd just picked from a tree.

'Now, eat this, we don't want you getting scurvy. Oh, and cheer up – I still love you, Cap'n.'

Hook sucked at his lemon. As juice ran down his stubbly chin, he replied, without once looking up, 'Love? You are truly disgusting, Smee.'

Now, I'd say that's a pretty rude way to speak to someone who's looking after you, but Smee was used to it. In fact, nothing Hook could say or do to him ever got him down. Every snide remark was just water off a duck's back to Smee. His loyalty to Hook was total.

Smee was like the most loyal pet dog: no matter how badly he was treated, he still loved his master unconditionally. And secretly – although of course he'd never admit it – Smee was the only person in his life that Hook had feelings for.

You might think that Mr Smee was an idiot – but far from it. If Smee was guilty of anything, it was of being an eternal optimist. And also, he'd never forgotten what Hook had done for him many, many years before. Smee had been on the original boat that Hook had captured and then turned into a pirate ship when they sailed to Neverland for the very first time. Smee, a petty crook, had left London to escape a humdrum life – or, as others say, to avoid being arrested and flung in jail. Being a kind but simple soul, Smee was initially laughed at, then bullied, by the other men on board.

Hook, who was far nicer in those days, took Smee under his wing and protected him. But it was the following incident that made Smee dedicate the rest of his life to his new captain. One night, during a violent storm, Smee was tossed overboard. As he thrashed around in twenty-foot waves, most of the crew were quite happy to let him drown. To be fair, one pirate did half-heartedly throw him a life ring, but Smee couldn't catch it. When Smee went under for the fourth – and potentially last – time, James Crook – yes, that was his original name – at full risk to his own life and to the astonishment of the other men on board, jumped into that swollen sea and dragged Smee back onto the boat. Hook saved his life, and Smee would never forget that.

'My head's sore Smee, too much sun. Damn this sun, does it never go away?'

Hook let out a howl of pain as Smee slapped a handful of sweet coconut water onto his bald head and rubbed.

'Hush now, this stuff always does the trick.'

As Smee massaged the soothing liquid into Hook's scalp, he hummed an old pirate tune and Hook reminisced.

'Ah, Smee . . . where did it all go wrong? Where? I had everything. I ruled Neverland . . .'

Between you and me, that's not entirely true, but it's what Hook believed. The funny thing was that just about everyone believed that they 'ruled' Neverland. Hook did, Peter Pan and the Lost Boys did. But the Opacanta tribe, the original humans on Neverland, who live in the island's north, no doubt had the strongest claim to the island.

As for the waters surrounding Neverland, that was disputed by no one, not even Hook, if he were being truthful. The mermaids ruled the waters.

Now, before you get misty-eyed and picture fun-loving creatures diving in and out of the water with their tails waving in the air, I must warn you, that's a myth. Mermaids are majestic, beautiful, flirty, mysterious, yet cunning and dangerous.

Protectors of their fellow sea creatures, these mermaids helped rescue turtles and stranded dolphins. They even attacked pirate boats which tried to harpoon whales – and they had lured many a pirate to a watery grave by enticing them in and dragging them under. Everyone was wary of them. Even Peter Pan. And for good reason. You needed eyes in the back of your head when it came to the mermaids of Neverland.

But the most dangerous inhabitants of Neverland were the witches. They lived in the 'No-No Zone' on the far west coast of the island, totally cut off from the inner jungles by huge, misty mountains, and they were pure evil. When they were selling their wares to the outside world, they looked just like sweet old ladies. But come darkness, they flew over Neverland looking for bodies, dead or alive. You could see them on a clear night, silhouetted against a starry sky. It was one of the last things a Lost Boy in his canopy tree-house could see as he dropped off to sleep. The Lost Boys were safe though – so far, the witches had failed in their efforts to discover the whereabouts of the Lost Boys' hideout.

Neverland may be beautiful, but with the wild animals in its dense forests and jungles, the chance of pirates finding you, mermaids who will drag you under if you get too close – or worse, witches – you definitely don't want to be outside after dark.

'I ruled Neverland, Smee . . .'

Smee humoured his captain, as always. 'Of course you did, Cap'n.'

'I had power, control and respect. And I finally had everything in my grasp. I was going to make those wretched Darling children walk the plank, starting with that annoying, sickly-sweet Wendy. But who comes to the rescue? Peter Pan, of course. Then I, James Hook, was made to walk my own plank!'

'Calm yourself, Cap'n, calm yourself.' Smee gently massaged Hook's temples as the old man continued his rant – the same rant he'd made every day for the last year.

'I hit the water like a brick, Smee, and that crocodile was waiting, waiting to gobble up old Hook. And it did, oh it did, Smee, and it was terrible.'

'I know Cap'n, I know.' Smee massaged harder.

'It swam away with me in its mouth, toying with me like a cat with a mouse. Then miles away, out at sea in the middle of nowhere, it spat me out, the ungrateful beast. How dare it spit out James Hook! Oh, the indignity.'

Smee raised his eyebrows and shook his head, not sure if the captain saw the irony in what he was saying.

'I was all at sea, Smee. But you – you picked me up in that little boat and brought me to safety.'

Hook got dewy-eyed as he recalled his life being saved, but it didn't last long, and he soon sounded bitter again as he continued ranting about being stuck on this damned island for eternity. He continued, 'And I bet Peter Pan and those wretched boys are enjoying themselves. Just imagine how much they're laughing at old Hook, laughing that he's dead. Yes, enjoying themselves and laughing, at my expense!'

CHAPTER 2

As another day began back in Neverland the Lost Boys, safe in their tree-houses deep in the inner jungle, were waking up. I guess it must be everyone's dream – to wake up when you want, no one nagging you to get out of bed, no school to go to, wear what you want, eat what you want. Heaven, right?

The Lost Boys used to think so, but not anymore.

'Good morning, Neverland!' bellowed Nibs as he stood out on the rope bridge directly outside his hut. It was the custom that each morning, one boy – they usually took it in turns – blasted out a good morning call on wakening, which kick-started another day of carefree adventure.

'Ah, shut up Nibs, it's too early. Go back to sleep!' Slightly grumbled in reply, before pulling his blanket over his head.

But it wasn't too early. They used to get up at dawn, and it was now mid-morning. Without pirates to chase, the Lost Boys were becoming lazy.

The original six Lost Boys had grown to sixteen over the years, but the current number was only eight, nine if you included Peter Pan. What had happened to those now missing from their ranks? Sadly, they weren't just missing.

The pirates had shot one, and made two walk the plank. The others had been killed by wild animals, and one Lost Boy – poor Snowy – was taken by witches.

The witches, as I explained earlier, flew over Neverland at night, looking for bodies. It wasn't actual flesh they were interested in, it was bones. They scooped up the bones – they'd take any dead creature, but humans were always the best – flew them back to the No-No Zone and boiled them up in enormous cauldrons.

The pirates used to supply the witches with a steady flow of dead bodies, usually from other ships they'd ransacked – though they also sold them the bodies of their fallen comrades.

The purpose of this grisly deed? From the gelatinous gloop of boiled-up bones, with added essential oils from Neverland's abundant plants, the witches made creams and lotions, which they bottled up, labelled 'organic' and sold to the inhabitants of surrounding islands, or to passengers on passing ships.

And of course, no customer ever knew what was actually in that nourishing face cream or foot balm.

A ghastly business indeed, but it made the witches plenty of money.

Oh yes, Neverland is a dangerous place, especially at night.

Slowly but surely, the surviving eight boys emerged from their hammocks. It may have been edging closer to midday, but it was breakfast time for them. It wasn't so long ago that they'd have gone for a two-mile run through the forest followed by a bracing swim in the waterfall before sitting down to breakfast. But for months they'd neglected exercise, apart from lifting their hands to their mouths to fill their stomachs.

The Lost Boys lived deep inside the inner forest in the middle of Neverland. Initially, they'd lived in huts on the ground, but decided it was too dangerous after one of them got mauled by a panther late one night. So, they built themselves a network of tree-houses. High up in the canopy, a series of rope bridges and walkways linked the huts together.

On the ground stood a thatched hut, with a roof but no walls, where the boys ate and cooked, and spent their time during daylight. But once it got dark, they always retreated up into the safety of their tiny tree-houses.

It had looked the same for years, but it was certainly much cleaner and tidier since Wendy visited Neverland. She had not been impressed by the mess, especially in the kitchen. But she soon got the boys whipped into shape and even made up a daily rota for cleaning, cooking and washing up. Naturally, they weren't too keen on being domesticated, but when Wendy threatened to stop telling them stories . . . they soon got used to their chores.

They missed Wendy. They missed her stories, her laugh, her kindness. She'd been a mother figure to them, the only mother most of them had ever known.

One by one, down the rope ladders they came and into their kitchen area.

'What's for breakfast?' yawned Slightly.

Nibs looked in the larder. 'Nothing . . .'

'How about honey?' asked Twin 1. 'I like honey.'

'We all like honey, but remember last time? I got stung, so it's not my turn,' said Tootles.

It was true: on their last honey hunt, Tootles had got himself stung badly. It was worth it, though – Neverland's bees made the purest, sweetest honey anyone was ever likely to taste.

'OK, I'll go,' said Twin 2. 'But someone make tea, and how about baking bread?'

'Deal,' they agreed, and set to work.

Their routine had changed, no doubt about that. In the days when they went for a run and a splash in their favourite waterfall first thing, they'd collect whatever took their fancy for breakfast on the way home.

And there was no shortage of choice. The boys liked to catch fish with spears made of sticks, especially rainbow trout. And they had their pick of fruits depending on the seasons. They loved coconuts, especially drinking the sweet water inside, but coconut picking often resulted in a lone coconut falling on someone – usually Slightly, who never believed it was an accident.

From the forests, the boys' favourite was blackberries and blueberries. They not only ate them, but also mashed them up and mixed them with herbs to make warpaint. They even made their own berry wine, from a recipe in a book they'd stolen from Pirate Cove. After all, there were no adults to tell them not to – although Tinkerbell, who had witnessed many a drunk pirate, rationed the wine. It was now only allowed on special occasions, and only with food.

What did the Lost Boys do all day?

They swung on vines and jumped into rivers, rode rapids in canoes and plunged down waterfalls. However, these days it was more about lying around eating berries until they felt they would burst. And there was food to catch – the Opacanta had taught them how to hunt game with a bow and arrow, and how to cook it – and of course they were always on their guard for pirates. Every day, the boys would go out in pairs to check the outskirts of their inner jungle.

The pirates were crude, and when they entered even the outer jungle, they'd hack away at everything in sight, so it was very easy to see if one had been in the area. A branch out of place, a twig snapped, or even a flower crushed, was all the boys needed to inform them that a pirate had been there recently.

And of course the boys, along with Peter and Tink, enjoyed nothing more than trying to infuriate the pirates as much as they could. Tink would fly into Pirate Cove, do her rounds, and report back to the boys, who would then make daring raids into the cove to either sabotage a boat or steal what they could.

One night after a successful raid, armed with a sack of flour to make bread, three wine goblets and one unfortunate pirate's wooden leg, they made their way back, but had left it too late. Under a clear night sky, they stood out like sore thumbs – easy for any passing witch to spot – and that was how poor Snowy met his end. Three of them swooped down on their brooms. This was the very first time the boys had ever come face to face with witches, and they were absolutely terrified.

They fought back bravely but, like so many hunters of prey, the witches focused on the weakest of the pack and singled out Snowy. As two witches swooped in and around the boys, causing panic and confusion, the third witch took her chance, grabbed Snowy by his white-blond hair, and flew off with him. Up into the night sky she flew, as Snowy screamed for help. Peter took to the skies and gave chase, all the way over Neverland, towards the mountains in front of the No-No Zone. But the witches were clever and the other two homed in on Peter, allowing the third, who had Snowy in her grasp, to fly off over the mountains.

Peter was desperate to go in and rescue Snowy, but Tink persuaded him not to.

'It's not safe, Peter. But I'm small enough, I'll go . . .' and off she flew.

Later that night, Peter and the boys were safely in their huts, eagerly waiting for Snowy's safe return. But Tink arrived alone.

The boys came rushing out of their huts onto the rope walkways.

'Well?' asked Peter.

Tink just shook her head and said, 'Sorry Peter, sorry boys . . .'

'What did you see there, Tink?' asked Tootles.

Tink said no more, just gave a look that implied *you really don't want to know*.

From then on, the boys couldn't raid Pirate Cove at night, because it was too dangerous – or in broad daylight either, because that was no fun – so they settled on dusk. They had a short window, but it was perfect timing as most of the pirates had gone to their tavern in the evenings to drink rum, leaving only one lookout who was easily distracted. The tavern in Pirate Cove had been converted from an old whaling station many years ago.

Three weeks later, they got their revenge on the witches. After a long debate about how to do it without putting any more of them in danger, they headed off early one evening. Finally, they stopped at a clearing in the jungle far enough away from their hideout and as close to the mountains as they dared to go.

Four of the boys each carried a yard-long hollowed-out bamboo cane. With a thick piece of cloth attached over the far end, they placed dozens of fireflies inside the cane and then covered the open end with a freshly spun spiders' web. The result created a powerful beam of light better than any torch.

The boys waited quietly until Tink, who was their lookout, spotted a witch.

'Witch overhead! Witch at twelve o'clock.'

'Go!' commanded Peter. The boys gave their bamboo canes a shake to wake up their fireflies, which lit up like a frenzy on the inside of the hollowed-out tubes. As one, the boys lifted their canes into the sky and aimed directly at their target.

Four intense beams of light hit the witch's eyes, and she instinctively took one hand off her broom and put it up to her face. Temporarily blinded, panicked and confused, she lost control of her broom, slammed into a thick nearby tree, and finally crashed to the ground in a crumpled heap.

* * *

Twin 2 was back from looting the wild bee colonies in the forest, and the boys were tucking into fresh honey, washed down with mugs of strong nettle tea. Since no one had bothered to make bread, it was just honey they ate, by the spoonful. Obi didn't even use a spoon, he just used his fingers.

'Where's Peter?' asked Nibs through a mouthful of honey.

'No idea,' said Zee. 'I didn't see him this morning. He got into bed last night though, I know that.'

'Anyone seen him?'

'He flew off once you boys were asleep,' said Tink, matter-of-factly.

'Where'd he go, Tink?'

'London, of course.'

'To visit Wendy again?'

'Who else?' said Tink, with a sneer. Tink had been thrilled when Wendy left Neverland and returned to London. But soon after the euphoria of Hook being gone forever had calmed down, Peter had started to fly to London again, just to look in on Wendy and her brothers, he said. *Yeah, right,* thought Tink. He always came back, but recently he was flying there more often and spending more time there than ever.

Tink was worried. She loved Peter, and was fiercely protective of him. But it seemed he was slowly drifting away from her, and there was nothing she could do to stop it. If she challenged him, it only pushed him further towards London.

Tinkerbell has the ability to make herself physically vanish and become a tiny glowing light; she does so to protect herself from being seen, especially if she's in and around Pirate Cove. She can't, though, sustain being a light for long, as it uses up way too much energy, and after a few minutes she automatically transfers back into full visible fairy form.

When she's only a light, she can communicate by a sound best described as a tinkling bell. This is real fairy language, and only Peter and three of the boys who have learned it can communicate with her this way. Of course, she can now speak English, taught to her by Peter a long time ago. She is clever and will happily do a deal with anyone she has to, to get the result she wants.

There used to be lots of fairies in Neverland, but they died out long ago and Tink is the only known survivor. She hasn't seen another fairy for years, which is something that causes her deep pain. It is said that every time a child somewhere in the outside world says, 'I don't believe in fairies,' a fairy drops down dead.

Tink, though, is not convinced by this tale, and believes that the demise of Neverland's fairies is due to their being poisoned by witches. The truth is, no one knows for sure what happened to Neverland's fairies – so please, I urge you not to tempt fate, and never say *I don't believe in fairies*, because they do exist, and they need our help to replenish their numbers.

The inner jungles of Neverland are so dense that much of the island is literally unexplored. With thick jungle and hidden caves, even the Lost Boys have not yet trodden every stone of Neverland. It is Tink's long-held belief that other fairies do still exist, it's just that she is yet to find them. It is her number one aim in life, after keeping Peter Pan safe of course, that one day she will find them and be reunited with her own kind.

On occasions, Tink has believed she had found other fairies . . . only to be deeply disappointed when they turned out to be mere fireflies.

When she does find them, it's her wish for them to bond together and create havoc in the No-No Zone, driving the witches from Neverland forever.

With a tiny body and tiny little wings, Tinkerbell can easily fit into the palm of your hand. She is tomboyish, yet beautiful in her own way.

But she's not all sweetness and light. In fact, her behaviour often leaves much to be desired. She is mischievous, cunning and totally loyal to Peter Pan. Her love for Peter is different from Wendy's, but she loves him nonetheless. The love you'd get with a mother, or sister, or a best friend who would die for you.

Tink is very wary of anyone getting too close to Peter, and of course was intensely jealous of Wendy when Peter first brought her to Neverland. But after a rocky start, she grew to like her, despite the fact she was – and still is – convinced Wendy had ulterior motives and secretly wanted Peter to leave Neverland, grow up and marry her.

'Not if I have any say in the matter,' she likes to remind the boys, the mermaids and anyone who will listen to her.

'I miss the old days,' said Tootles.

Like politicians sitting in parliament, they all grumbled their agreement.

'I miss our fights with the pirates. They were so easy to beat, so easy to steal from, so easy to sabotage,' added Nibs. 'We had so many victories.'

'But they don't want to fight anymore,' said Zee, which got another round of grumbling agreement.

Suddenly, Slightly said, 'I miss Hook!'

Everyone gasped.

'Are you crazy?'

'No – think about it. Ever since Hook was killed, we've not exactly been happy, have we?'

He was right, of course.

'What if . . .'

'What if what?'

'What if Hook isn't dead?'

'Don't be stupid, the croc swallowed him, remember? We all saw it – it took him in its mouth and dragged him away to eat him.'

Slightly wasn't convinced though. 'But what if Hook somehow managed to escape? We never saw blood or guts, and no remains of him have washed ashore, or the mermaids would have told us.'

'Nah, not possible . . .' Curly dismissed such thoughts.

They all thought about it for a moment or two – but no, it wasn't possible. Twin 2 scratched his chin. *What strange times we live in,* he thought. *We've only just got rid of Hook and now we want him back . . .*

Tink was suddenly intrigued. It was a valid point. None of them had actually seen Hook die and not even a scrap of his clothing had washed up on Neverland's shores. Could Hook still be alive?

'I'm off boys, catch you later,' she said, and off she flew through the trees, going in no particular direction.

Maybe old Hook is still alive after all . . . and maybe that's exactly what we need . . . thought Tink. *Time to do some investigating.*

CHAPTER 3

The Darlings' home in London was a typical West End terraced house of the time. For those with money, that is. The Darling family were not millionaires, but lived comfortably. Mr Darling worked hard to provide for his family, and he was a supporter of the class structure of British society, having worked his way successfully up the social ladder. This was Victorian England, after all.

It was now six months since her brothers Michael and John had left for boarding school, so Wendy had the run of the top floor of the house to herself.

Peter Pan sat perched on the balcony railing and peered in through the nursery window. He recalled the time more than a year ago when he'd been looking for his shadow. He'd visited the Darling house a few times before that evening; he loved to listen in as Wendy read stories to her brothers. But on that fateful night, the window had slammed shut, cutting his shadow clean off. Tink helped find it, but just as Peter was sitting on the nursery floor trying in vain to stick it back on with soap, Wendy had woken up.

And the rest, as they say, is history.

This time, Wendy wasn't asleep – she was in bed, reading.

As soon as she saw him, she slipped on her dressing gown and ran over to him.

'Peter! Oh, come in, I'm so glad to see you!'

Peter stepped in through the window and into the warmth of the nursery. He took in the now very familiar surroundings and smiled. He liked it here. It felt . . . what was that feeling? Homely.

They hugged, which Peter made a fuss of. He found it awkward, as most boys do, but secretly he loved it.

They sat on the edge of Wendy's bed and smiled at each other. Peter had always thought Wendy pretty, but it was only during these past few visits that he'd realised she was not just pretty, she was beautiful.

Her long, light-brown hair fell down over her right shoulder, and was tied in a single bunch, while her brown eyes brimmed with innocence and kindness.

They sat and talked for over an hour, nothing of any real importance, just catching up on each other's lives. Suddenly and unexpectedly, Wendy said, 'Stay, Peter – stay the night. Mother and Father won't mind.'

True, her parents wouldn't mind, not one bit. Big changes had taken place in the Darling household, especially in Mr Darling, who used to be rather stuffy. Being a product of the class system he lived under, it would be harsh to say it was all his fault. He was a kind man but, having a very British stiff upper lip, Mr Darling wanted an end to childhood games and had even suggested that Wendy should leave the nursery and sleep in her own room. He'd said at the time, 'I think it's time for you to grow up, young lady' – and that was what had led to Wendy and her brothers taking off for Neverland. But on her return, after being fraught with worry, Mr Darling mellowed, and came to accept that he should not force his daughter to grow up before her time. 'Stay in the nursery as long as you like, my dear,' he said. These days, Wendy and her father were closer than they had ever been.

As for not growing up, the opposite was happening. Since Neverland, Wendy was growing up fast, all by herself. She knew it. She even had a strange tingling in her stomach that told her she might be falling in love with Peter.

Peter was often immature and stubborn. But he was also handsome, fearless and brave. He'd flown her to Neverland, where she'd had the adventure of a lifetime, before returning her to the safety of her family. Despite having no regrets over leaving Neverland, Wendy was delighted when Peter came to visit.

Before Peter was able to give his answer about spending the night, Wendy called out, 'Mother! Father! Peter's here!'

* * *

Sitting round the kitchen table, Peter and Wendy were drinking hot chocolate and eating Mrs Darling's home-made oat and honey biscuits. 'Delicious,' Peter told her, which pleased Mrs Darling immensely.

'Why don't you stay, Peter, it's bitterly cold out,' said Mrs Darling. 'You can sleep in John's bed, then fly back to Neverland in the morning.'

In her head, Wendy said, *Stay, stay for ever, stay here and let's grow up together*. But she didn't dare say it out loud – it would send Peter running a mile.

To everyone's surprise, Peter accepted the offer. He was enjoying the warmth and kindness in the Darling household. It was worth the bother – and by that he meant that he knew Tink would give him a hard time when he got back to Neverland.

He accepted John's bed, but point-blank refused to take a bath, even though Nana tried her best to drag him into the tub. Nana, a big, shaggy, white English sheepdog, looked after the Darling children. At first, this had been very hard for Mr Darling to accept. 'A dog for a nanny? But what will the people at the bank think?'

'Oh George, don't be so stuffy. Nana is a treasure,' his wife constantly told him. It took some getting used to, and it drove him mad when Nana accidentally brushed up against him and covered his good trousers in dog hair. But in time, he accepted her.

'Oh Peter, you are funny,' Wendy commented as he struggled with Nana on the landing.

Finally, Peter got into John's bed. To Wendy's surprise, he even let Mrs Darling tuck him in. Peter liked her, she was kind, as a mother should be. She kissed him on the forehead and quietly closed the door.

'Goodnight, Peter,' whispered Wendy from her bed at the other side of the room. 'Sleep well, sleep deep.'

'Goodnight, Wendy,' said a sleepy but happy Peter. As he drifted off inside his warm, cosy and comfy bed, his mind drifted to Neverland and the boys bedding down in their tree-houses. Did he miss them? No, he admitted to himself, he didn't.

He felt safe here, he felt good here. What did Neverland have to offer him now? For the first time in his life, he didn't have an answer to that question. An enormous wave of tiredness finally washed over him and he soon fell into a deep and dreamless sleep.

An hour later, Mr Darling popped his head round the

door to check in on them. All was calm. When he was fast asleep, with his innocent face, Peter looked like any other boy. And his beautiful daughter Wendy, she seemed to be smiling in her sleep. Mr Darling believed, as most fathers did in those days, that he should always be on the lookout for a young man who could take over and marry his daughter. Someone to look after and protect her.

It may sound old-fashioned, but that's how it was in those days.

Mr Darling looked over at Peter once more. He was an unusual boy, and that was putting it mildly. But against his better judgement, he had come to realise that no matter what, his precious daughter would always be safe as long as Peter Pan was in her life. Mr Darling closed the door gently and let them sleep.

Tiny specks of light twinkled on the nursery ceiling, reflections of the stars just outside the window, as the two inhabitants of the nursery slept peacefully.

Just as well that Tink wasn't there to witness it – she'd have been seething with jealousy.

CHAPTER 4

Hook was sitting under his makeshift sunshade. He tended not to venture out much during the day; it was far too hot for him. Getting sunburnt gave him no pleasure whatsoever.

Smee had been spear fishing – not in the sea, but in a small freshwater lagoon a little way inland. He'd caught an armful of fish, which he planned to cook later, over an open fire. 'Fish for tea, tasty fish for tea,' Smee cheerily sang to himself as he headed back to camp.

As Smee came out of the bush and walked along the hot sand towards their hut, he once again took in the sight of his captain, sitting alone with his head bowed. He'd tried everything to get him to buck up, but without success. As he got closer, Smee could see that he was fiddling with a small chain around his neck. Attached to the chain, a silver locket.

This wasn't new behaviour – Smee used to notice it every morning as he was getting Hook dressed on the *Jolly Roger*. He even slept with it, only taking it off when he had a bath. Smee had never asked him about it; it wasn't any of his business. It was only a locket.

For years, Hook had absently toyed with the locket between thumb and forefinger. But now, every day they'd been stranded on this small island, it was Hook's sole focus. He'd touch it, rub it, open the locket and stare at it. Then touch it and rub it again and again. What on earth was it? *Time to ask*, thought Smee.

'Fish for tea, tasty fish for tea,' sang Smee with a smile as he dumped a pile of fresh wet fish on the sand directly in front of Hook. Hook kept fiddling with his locket, and didn't look up.

'What is it, Cap'n? What's the story behind that locket? Tell your old pal Smee.'

He was expecting a telling-off for asking, a mouthful of something like 'mind your own business'. But no, not this time. There is, as they say, a time and a place for everything, and this, right now, was the time. Hook even looked relieved as he unburdened his story to Smee.

'I was never loved, Smee.'

'I love you, Cap'n.'

'Smee . . .'

Smee knew what that look meant. 'Shall I shut up, Cap'n?'

'Correct . . . My mother abandoned me, Smee, if you can call her that. I had a twin brother, and well, the story I was told was that my father ran off, leaving my mother with two boys to bring up alone. She'd barely enough money to feed herself, let alone two children. So she decided to give one of us up. And that was me. But why me, Smee? I guess because she didn't love me. She abandoned me, left me in a basket outside Great Ormond Street Hospital in London. I spent the first eight years of my life being passed from pillar to post – orphanages, and even the poor house, which I eventually ran away from.'

'Where did you live, Cap'n?'

'On the streets, Smee, the cold, hard streets of London. No childhood for me. How could any mother abandon her child, then never give him a second thought? She was no mother. She had no heart.

'This locket,' he said, holding it up, 'is all I have left, Smee. Mother . . .' he said sarcastically, 'left it round my neck when she abandoned me.'

'What's in it Cap'n, a picture of her?'

'No, one of me as a baby, and in the other half a picture of what I believe is my older twin brother.' Smee watched as Hook's mind drifted. 'I've often wondered what became of him.' Then, in a voice as soft as Smee had ever heard, 'And what became of my mother.'

Hook snapped out of it, and he made Smee jump as he barked, 'Enough of this sentimental mush! Get that fish on the fire, Smee, I'm hungry.'

Smee gutted the fish with his trusty knife, but he wanted the rest of the story, which Hook then told – in a non-sentimental way.

'From the age of eight I was forced to grow up fast, Smee. It was all about survival. I spent a couple of years living with a pack of other young boys. An old man let us stay in his squat down by the docks at the River Thames, and he taught us to steal. We gave him what we stole and in return he fed and took care of us. It wasn't so bad – at least it resembled something of a family. Through my teenage years, I lived where I could. I got into trouble with the police, spent time in jail even. Finally, I decided I was done with London, so I jumped on a cargo ship – bound for the West Indies, if I recall correctly.'

'On that ship, Cap'n, that's where we met.'

'Correct, Smee.'

'Then after months at sea, half-starving and going nowhere, we had a mutiny, and we took over the ship.'

'*I* took over the ship, Smee,' corrected Hook, with huge emphasis on the *I*.

'And we became pirates, and the fun began. We stole from other ships and finally landed up on a paradise island. Neverland. And we met Peter Pan.'

'And I ruled Neverland.'

'Course you did, Cap'n, course you did. And the rest, as they say, is history!' Smee smiled proudly at himself for saying something so clever.

Hook wasn't that impressed. He grunted, 'Fish, Smee! Cook those damn fish!'

CHAPTER 5

Dawn had broken and Neverland was slowly waking up to yet another spectacular day. Peter had only just arrived back from his night in London and was enjoying a moment of peace and calm at Mermaid Lagoon before visiting Tink and the boys.

Wendy had still been asleep when he left. Pan had even considered giving her a kiss, but quickly dismissed the idea. I mean, kissing wasn't for boys – not him, anyway. Now, though, as he sat on his rock and contemplated another uneventful day ahead, he wished for the first time that he *had* kissed Wendy.

There were six mermaids out that morning in the bay. They looked so elegant and playful as they dived in and out of the water. Yet, Peter always had to remind himself that they could be unpredictable. Fierce, even. 'Keep your wits about you,' he told himself.

He'd never considered his own age. He was a boy, and that was that – but he often wondered how old the mermaids were. Migizi, the Opacanta chief, had told him that mermaids could live for up to two hundred years, yet they always remained young and beautiful. In fact, they never seemed to age.

'Good morning Peter Pan . . .'

'Good morning Ilba.'

Known to everyone as the mermaid leader, Ilba was stunning. A woman from head to waist, and fish from the waist down. She had long, flowing black hair, flawless skin and piercing blue eyes.

Ilba swam over to Peter and rested her arms and chin on the rock directly in front of him.

'What's up?'

'Oh, nothing much.'

'Where are you, Peter Pan?' she asked.

Peter thought it a stupid question.

'I'm sitting here, of course, right in front of you.'

'You may be physically here, but not up there you're not,' she said, pointing to his head.

'What d'you mean?'

'You're far away, your mind is somewhere else . . .'

If only she knew, thought Peter. Did she know, though? She was not only attractive, but also very clever indeed. Some people even believed that mermaids could read human minds.

'You are a free spirit, Peter, you never have to grow up, you live in paradise,' Ilba reminded him.

'I know, but it's just not the same without Hook. I can't believe I'm saying that, but it's true.'

Ilba, despite having no time for pirates, understood.

'You need to find a new focus, Peter.'

Ilba started to flirt, tracing a long, elegant wet finger down Peter's left arm. Her nails were sharp, yet Peter was surprised to find that he quite liked the sensation. However, a warning voice in his head reminded him she could draw blood at any moment if she wanted to. Peter carefully moved his arm out of her reach, which made her smile a knowing smile.

You won't be surprised to learn that Tink was very jealous of the mermaids, especially when they flirted with Peter.

'It's a new day, so be off with you, Peter Pan, go and find your focus.'

'You're right,' said Peter as he stood up. 'The thing is, though, I don't think I can find it in Neverland anymore.' And with that, off he flew towards the inner jungle and the Lost Boys.

Ilba backed off into the water, letting her gaze follow Peter high in the sky until he was out of sight. Then she slipped under the water and vanished.

After leaving Mermaid Lagoon, Peter enjoyed a flight over Neverland. As he gazed down over his island, he couldn't help admiring it. Yet London, which he'd left only a few hours before, had beauty too, in its own way. Or was that just a certain young lady in the Darling household?

Peter flew north over the Opacanta settlement. Small fires crackled in a clearing by the northern beaches. The Opacanta, of course, had been up since dawn.

Peter swooped down and landed on the beach. From a distance, he watched them go about their business. They were a quiet people. They didn't waste precious energy with idle chit-chat. Women cooked breakfast, others washed clothes, while men stood fishing in the sea and children played in the grass.

They looked so happy and contented. *Why can't I be happy?* Peter mused.

'Peter . . . come.'

The quiet voice of the Opacanta chief beckoned Peter over to the front of his modest hut. Long ago, Peter had simply called him 'chief'. However, once a bond had been formed between the two, the old man had told him his name was Migizi, which means eagle.

Migizi handed Peter a chunk of warm flatbread that moments ago had come out of a huge clay oven. Everyone knew the Opacanta made the tastiest bread ever. Despite many lessons from none other than the chief's wife Aki, the Lost Boys had yet to fully master the art of bread making.

Peter thanked Migizi and sat opposite him. He ripped at the warm bread and shoved an enormous chunk greedily into his mouth. He was hungry after flying back from London. Peter often wondered how long it took him. But like the Opacanta, he had no practical use for clock time. He guessed the flight took him a few hours, and there must be a time difference between London and Neverland, because even when he left London at dawn, he would arrive in Neverland around dawn. *Funny thing, time*, Peter thought to himself. *Quite a mystery, really.*

'You are troubled,' came the words from the old man.

'Oh, it's nothing, I'm fine,' Peter replied, trying to sound upbeat.

Migizi nodded, though he didn't believe a word of it. He'd been observing Peter over the long months since Hook's death, and it was obvious to him that the boy was troubled.

He didn't need to ask again; he just looked at Peter, who could tell the old man knew he was unhappy. Through mouthfuls of warm bread, Peter said, 'Ilba told me something this morning. She said I need to find my focus.'

The chief paused before replying. In fact, the chief always paused to think before saying anything, but especially before replying.

'Ilba is wise, listen to her.'

'What's your secret, Migizi? Your people are content here. But I don't feel it anymore. What can I do to make myself happy? I fly, I play – but I just can't find the happiness I used to have.'

Another pause before the reply came. 'You must look inside, young Peter. Happiness does not come from outside, only from in here,' said the chief, touching his own chest.

'But . . .'

'Look inside, Peter, and listen to what you find. We each must look into our hearts, for only there will we find where our future lies.' And with that, Migizi turned away and focused on his people going about their lives. He could sit and observe them for hours and speak not a word.

Peter realised it was his cue to leave, but before he got up, he crammed another chunk of warm bread into his mouth.

He flew back over Mermaid Lagoon, where Ilba and her fellow mermaids were now lying out on the rocks. They could only sunbathe until late morning – after that they were in danger of drying out. He swooped down and over the mermaids, who all waved at him, beckoning him to come closer. But Peter knew better than to place himself in such proximity to a whole gaggle of mermaids. He smiled, shook his head and kept flying. But he had to admit he'd been tempted.

Tink liked to tell him that if he ever kissed a mermaid, only then would he discover their true nature.

'What do you mean, Tink?'

'Well, they may seem *somewhat* beautiful,' she reluctantly said, 'but if you ever actually kissed one . . . they'd turn into hideously ugly catfish! The ugliest, slimiest catfish you've ever seen! Then, they'd swallow you whole!'

'Rubbish!' said Peter.

'No, it's true! But of course if you don't believe me, go and kiss one, then you'll find out . . .'

Tink was cunning, and she knew exactly what she was doing. As mesmerised as Peter was with the mermaids (especially Ilba, as he secretly told Tootles one night when he thought no one was listening), he'd never kiss one, just in case she did turn into an ugly, slimy, hideous catfish.

Tink, hiding in a nearby tree, had overheard the conversation and had to stop herself laughing out loud. *Boys are so easy to fool*, she thought.

Peter swooped in and out over the outer forest. He was ready now to fly straight to the inner jungle and the Lost Boys' hideout, but something pulled him in the opposite direction. No, not towards the No-No Zone – after what the witches had done to Snowy, he never flew over there, even in daylight.

Instead, Peter turned in mid-air and flew south, over Pirate Cove. Even this early in the morning, it used to be teeming with pirates. Some would be getting the *Jolly Roger* loaded up for another trip out onto the high seas, either to rob other passing ships, or to hunt. Others would be organising a group to head into the jungle for yet another pointless attempt at finding the boys' secret hideout. Peter smiled, remembering so many adventures. He loved tackling the pirates, they were so useless and so easy to beat. But this morning, Pirate Cove was deathly quiet.

Peter landed quietly on the deck of the *Jolly Roger*. The boat itself, once the pirates' pride and joy, had certainly seen better days. Ships are very much like human bodies: they must be tended to regularly, or they eventually fall apart. There were rips in the sails, the odd missing plank of wood on the deck, and the sides were being taken over by barnacles. And strangely, the famous pirate flag, the skull and crossbones, was nowhere to be seen . . .

Peter walked up the steps to Hook's old cabin, which had one smashed window and two cracked ones. He peered inside. Not much to see, as anything of value had already been stripped out and used elsewhere. It all looked very sad. He turned around, standing where Hook once used to stand to face his men and bark his orders for the day. As Peter placed his hand on the banister, he felt a rough edge to the wood. He looked at it and smiled a sad smile when he realised what it was. Slash marks from Hook's hook.

Hook had been his greatest enemy, a dangerous man who wanted him dead. Peter had long fought against Hook, and finally he'd won. Yet he'd never imagined it ending the way it did. Peter had just wanted to constantly get the better of him, even humiliate him. When Hook fell off his own plank and that croc swallowed him, everyone was full of joy. Even some of the pirates, if truth be told.

But he'd never actually pictured a Neverland without him.

As Peter ran his smooth hand over the rough marks on the wood made by the hook, he quietly admitted to himself, 'I miss our battles, Hook.'

He snorted at his own words. Was he going mad?

Suddenly he heard the most awful noise, a deep, guttural sound like a wild animal. Peter's hand went straight to the small dagger he always carried in his belt, but then he spotted the source, slumped behind a barrel. A snoring pirate. A pirate sleeping off yet another drunken night. A half-empty bottle of rum lay across his lap. Peter kicked it away and with his best Hook impersonation, barked, 'Get up on your feet, my man!'

The pirate roused, half-opening his eyes. Peter, now standing beyond his eyeline, continued, 'Stand to attention when addressed by your captain!'

The poor man sobered up quickly, thinking Hook had miraculously returned. He staggered to his feet and saluted towards the captain's quarters.

Peter roared with laughter and the pirate spun round to face him.

'That's a cruel trick to play, Pan.'

'Come on then, fight me, Mr Edwards,' challenged Peter.

Edwards scratched at his beard, his eyes not yet properly focused. 'Nah,' he said, and dismissed Peter with a flick of his hand.

'C'mon, you coward, go and get your men and take on Peter Pan. If you dare!'

Edwards sat down on the deck with his back against the barrel.

'You don't get it, do you, Pan? Hook's dead. It's over, and it has been for a long time.' He then said something that struck home. 'But don't think you won, Pan, for you didn't. You're as miserable as we are. Even more so.'

Edwards picked up the rum bottle, took a swig and wiped his mouth with the back of his hand before adding, 'Leave me alone . . . beat it, Pan!'

Shocked, Peter flew off. Edwards was right – he, Pan, had won nothing.

As he soared over Neverland, he once again heard Ilba's voice in his head. *Find your focus, Peter Pan . . .*

* * *

'Hey boys, Peter's back! Peter's back!' shouted Nibs.

The boys looked up as Peter landed on the ground beside them. The questions came thick and fast.

'What's up, Peter?'

'How was London?'

'Did you see Wendy?'

'Did she read you a story?'

'Everything's fine boys, I'll fill you in later.' He turned to Tink. 'Hey, Tink, what's up around here?'

'Not much . . .'

'Exactly,' replied Peter.

'Are you hungry Peter? We've got honey!' exclaimed Zee.

'No, thanks, I ate with Migizi earlier.'

'Let's go to Pirate Cove and cause some havoc!'

'Yeah, great idea, we could . . .'

'Don't waste your time. I've been there this morning, there's no one around. The place is dead.'

'Did you see the mermaids today, Peter?'

'Yes, just come from there.'

Tink scrunched up her nose as she observed the boys go all doe-eyed at the mention of mermaids. 'Remember what I told you boys . . . one kiss, and bam! Hideous ugly catfish.'

The boys shook their heads and shivered, and again Tink had to stifle a laugh.

'So what are we going to do today, Peter?' asked the twins at the same time.

'No idea, Twins.'

'But we're bored.'

'And what do you want me to do about it?'

'You're our leader . . .'

'Hey! What's the game?' cried Slightly. Pan was gently poking him in the stomach with a stick.

'When did you get so fat, Slightly?' Peter teased.

'I'm not!' he replied, a bit too defensively.

Peter looked around and for the first time noticed that all his Lost Boys were on the plump side.

'Come on, Peter, decide what we're going to do today.'

'Why me?'

'Because you're our leader,' the twins called out again.

Maybe I don't want to be your leader anymore, Peter thought, but obviously he didn't actually say it. Instead he lay down on a nearby hammock and closed his eyes, claiming he was tired after his night flight.

'What's up with him, Tink?' whispered Obi.

Tink replied solemnly, 'We're losing him, that's what.'

'What do you mean?'

'Haven't you noticed? He spends most of his time flying to London and back.'

'Doesn't Peter care about us anymore?' asked Nibs.

'Of course he does, it's just . . . just . . .'

'Just what?'

'I don't know,' she grumbled.

* * *

Later that day, Peter and Tink were sitting on a branch at the very top of one of Neverland's tallest trees, looking out over miles of lush green jungle.

'What's up, Peter? Why so sad?'

'There's nothing left for me here, Tink.'

'How can you say that?'

Peter shrugged.

'It's her, isn't it?'

'Who?'

'Wendy Moira Angela Darling.' Tink's words dripped with sarcasm.

'Oh, give it up Tink.'

'She's filled your head with all kinds of nonsense about growing up.'

'Leave it, Tink.'

'Everything was perfect, until you brought her and her brothers here.'

'She has a name, Tink,' said Peter defensively.

'I know, *Wendy Moira Angela Darling.*'

'Stop it, Tink.'

Tink decided to change tack.

'We have everything here, Peter. Look around you; this is paradise. OK, we've still got to watch out for witches – but come on, we can do what we want all day, and no adults to tell us otherwise.'

'I know, but . . .'

'But what? You miss the adventures?'

'Yeah.'

'So we can make more. There are still pirates to fight, and we can cause so much trouble for them. Remember the time . . .'

'It's not enough, Tink, not anymore. I feel different inside, it's like something's missing. Ilba said I need to find my focus.'

'You didn't kiss her, did you?'

'No!'

'That's all right then. What are you looking for, Peter?'

'I don't know, Tink, but whatever it is, I don't think I'll find it here.' Peter stood up, breathed in and out slowly, and gazed off into the distance.

'You're heading off again, aren't you? Where are you going, if I need ask?'

Peter said nothing. Tink kept at him.

'You're going to London, aren't you?'

'Yes, yes I am.'

'You're abandoning the Lost Boys, Peter.'

'No, I'm not!'

'You are, and you know it,' said Tink, wagging a small but stern finger. 'You're everything to them, Peter. They love you, they look up to you. You're their leader.'

'Maybe I don't want to be their leader anymore!' he blurted out.

Tink was shocked, but refrained from saying anything that might cause a huge row. She just shook her head with disappointment.

Peter was uncomfortable, guilty even. 'Don't do that, Tink.' Not wanting this conversation to continue any longer he added, 'I need to get out of here. I'll see you later, OK?'

Tink turned her head away from him and replied, 'Do what you want, Peter Pan, seems you're going to anyway.'

Tink had an awful feeling deep inside. They were in danger of losing Peter. But what to do? She knew he was unhappy, but nothing she suggested to cheer him up worked anymore. How can you fight against what someone's feeling? No doubt he was falling in love with Wendy and there was little she could do about that – the last thing she wanted was to push him even further away.

She had to find something that would persuade him to stay in Neverland. Something that meant more to him than the lure of London. But what? Playing tricks on pirates? No. Spending the days enjoying being a boy with no responsibilities? No, not anymore.

Then what? What meant more to Peter Pan than anything else?

It didn't take her long to work out the answer; a one-word answer.

Hook.

CHAPTER 6

Tink was as wary as anyone when it came to mermaids. Maybe even more so. No one really knew what food mermaids ate, but Tink guessed that insects were probably part of their diet, and the last thing she wanted as she hovered over the lagoon was to be mistaken for a mosquito and swallowed whole.

Tink stayed a safe height from the water's surface as she darted around looking for mermaids. Suddenly, like a dolphin breaching, a mermaid came out of the water right under her, causing her to back off. The figure leapt at least six feet in the air, twisted and turned and dived back under before resurfacing. The face had a totally waterproof olive shine to it, the eyes a striking blue. Ilba.

'Good evening, Tinkerbell. What brings you here?'

Even Tink grudgingly accepted that Ilba was attractive. In fact, she was beyond beauty. What boy wouldn't want to kiss her? Or girl, for that matter.

'It's Peter, he's not happy. I need to help him, but don't know how. Has he confided in you?'

'Yes, we've talked.'

'And?'

'He needs adventure again. Life is not the same in Neverland for him anymore.'

'I know that already, Ilba.'

'He needs a new focus . . .'

'Fancy words, but no meaning.'

Ilba smiled. 'You're scared you're going to lose him, aren't you?'

It would have been easy for Tink to get defensive and argue with her, but instead she chose to hold her tongue.

'Yes . . . I am. But I don't know what to say to him. Nothing seems to work anymore – I can't get through to him. I need to give him some hope that he has a future here.'

Ilba momentarily dipped her head under the water. Mermaids did this constantly, to keep themselves hydrated. If anything, it made them even more alluring. With fresh water dripping off the end of her perfectly sculpted nose she said, 'Hope, is it? Well, I might be in a position to help you there . . .'

'What do you mean?'

'Go and speak with the Opacanta, they know much more than I do.'

'What is it? What do you know, Ilba?'

'I'm not sure, but I've heard rumours. Something's up . . .'

'Are you helping me here, or are you playing games as usual?'

'No games, Tink, but it's not for me to say. Go and speak with the Opacanta.' She slipped under the water and vanished, making Tinkerbell shiver.

* * *

Minutes later, after flying north-west, Tink arrived at the settlement.

The Opacanta as usual were quietly going about their business, the women busy preparing evening meals while men tended fires on the beaches.

Tink flew over to the chief. Sitting outside his hut, he was enjoying the sunset. She landed on his right shoulder.

'Migizi?'

Tink might have been small, but her voice, especially when she was excited or wound up, was anything but delicate.

'Migizi!' she said even louder, as she tugged at his ear. She flitted down to his knee, and with her hands on her hips and a face like a grumpy teenager, she waited for a response.

'I heard you the first time, little Bell,' he said calmly. 'What can I do for you?'

'Ilba told me you had news, something about rumours? What's going on?'

'There are reports of strange happenings.'

'On Neverland? Is it the witches? Are they planning an attack?'

'No . . .'

She respected Migizi and his ability to always stay relaxed, but she wished he'd get to the point.

'Then what? What strange happenings?'

'Smoke signals . . . Two nights ago . . .'

'From where?'

'From the Meshot tribe on their island to the east of Wanallah.'

'Wanallah?'

'Your so-called Neverland, Miss Bell.'

Tink had forgotten, and cursed herself for sounding disrespectful. Neverland was a white man's name. To the

Opacanta, it had always been and would always be known as Wanallah.

'What did the smoke signals say?'

'They say . . .'

'Yes . . .'

'They say that they have spotted two white men on a small deserted island some ten miles to their east.'

Now that is strange, thought Tink. 'Shipwreck? Lost sailors from a cargo ship?'

'Maybe . . .'

'You're worried, I can tell. What are you not telling me?'

'The Meshot say that the flag of the *Jolly Roger*, the skull and crossbones, is flying from a palm tree on the beach.'

'How can that be? It's not possible.'

'Oh, everything is possible.'

'Two white men, you say?'

'That's what I read in the smoke, yes.'

'Any more description?'

'No.'

She turned to Migizi, who now had his eyes closed. He was meditating as dusk settled on Wanallah. 'Do you think it's Hook? Do you think he could still be alive?'

The chief sat in silence for a long ten seconds before opening his eyes and speaking to her in his ever-calm voice. 'Everything is possible.'

'I've got to go . . . oh, and thanks, thanks for the news!' With that, Tink flew off at great speed. Migizi inhaled and exhaled deeply as he contemplated the rushing-around of others. *Not good for the digestion, not good for the soul,* he liked to tell his people.

Tink flew straight back to Mermaid Lagoon, found Ilba and told her she'd spoken with Migizi, before asking what she remembered about the day Hook disappeared.

'Soon after the crocodile took Hook, we followed Mr Smee out of the bay for two miles or so.'

'Tell me more.'

'He headed off in a small rowing boat, in search of Hook.'

'Did he find him?'

'I don't know, but we saw no remains of Hook. No chewed-up, spat-out bits . . . so it's possible.'

'Tell me, did Smee carry anything with him in that boat?'

'Only a small bag. Food I'd guess, or possibly a gun.'

'Why didn't you tell me this a year ago?'

'I didn't think it important,' Ilba replied.

Tink forced herself to stay calm. 'Fair enough. Was Smee carrying anything else?'

Ilba thought long and hard before replying, 'The flag of the *Jolly Roger*.'

Tink's face lit up. 'Really? You saw it?'

'Yes, why?'

Tink explained in detail what the chief had said about smoke signals, two white men and the flag.

'You think he's still alive, don't you Tinkerbell?'

'I . . . I . . . I don't know, but it's possible. What do you think?'

'Unlikely, but who knows? Want me to find out? We can swim around tomorrow and see if we can spot anything.'

Tink wanted to blurt out 'yes', but paused. 'No, not yet. I need to speak to the Lost Boys first. Thank you, Ilba.'

'You're welcome, Tinkerbell. You'd better be off now, it's getting dark, the witches will be out soon.' She said this with a sly, unnerving smile.

Tink decided to take Ilba's advice and make her way back to the safety of the hideout.

CHAPTER 7

'You've never told me the proper story, Father. You always said you'd explain when I was older. Well, I'm older now.'

Mr Darling looked at his daughter. No doubt she was growing up fast, yet still so innocent in many ways. He had wanted to shield her from the cruel realities of life, but now he felt she deserved the truth.

'You're right my dear.' He patted the sofa, and waited till Wendy was sitting comfortably.

'My father, who I never knew, left my mother. He left her with no money and two children.'

'*Two* children?' Wendy thought she'd misheard.

'Yes, myself and my twin brother. Baby James. I still think of him as that, baby James, even to this day. It must have been heart-breaking for Mother, but she couldn't keep both of us. I was older and fitter, so I suppose she thought I was more likely to survive. My brother had a bad chest and a weak left side, from what I can remember. After what must have been an agonising decision for her, Mother wrapped baby James in a blanket, along with a bottle, a note and a locket, rang the bell, and left him on the steps of Great Ormond Street Hospital.'

'Oh, how awful.'

'Yes . . . But I urge you not to judge her, Wendy, it was devastating for her. I saw the effect it had on her for many years. It haunted her. My mother, your grandmother Masie Crook, died when you were very young. Do you remember her, Wendy?'

'Yes, she was a kind lady. But now I think of it, she always seemed sad.'

'She was sad. And even though she went on to remarry – your Grandpa Darling, my stepfather – allowing me, and later you, a new surname, she never got over being forced to give up her youngest child all those years ago.'

Mr Darling took a small locket attached to a silver chain out of his wallet. He opened the locket and presented it to his daughter. Inside there were two old, faded black and white photographs of two little boys.

'Who are they, Father?'

'That's me,' he pointed to the photo on the right. 'And here on the left is baby James.'

'What happened to him?'

'No one knows. Mother regretted her decision for the rest of her life. She spent years trying to find him. I tried too – I've looked at the records of poor houses, orphanages, even placed adverts in newspapers and magazines, but to no avail. I've spent countless hours walking the poor areas of London, just looking, looking for my brother – who of course is now my age, so I have no idea what he looks like today. Stupid of me, really.'

'It's not, Father. You were brave and kind to try and find him. And I don't blame Grandmother either.'

'Thank you, Wendy, that brings me comfort.' He got up, walked over to the fireplace, and prodded the dying embers with the poker.

'He's probably dead by now. James, that is. Possibly a long time ago, maybe even in childhood. They were harsh times indeed.' He paused.

'Thank you for listening to me, Wendy. It has helped. And you know something else? I think it's time for me to move on. The past is the past. James is long gone, I just pray he's in a better place.'

But Mr Darling knew that deep down, he'd never give up hope that one day he'd find his long-lost baby brother.

CHAPTER 8

Neverland's witches numbered four. Four too many, according to everyone else. There were originally five, until Peter made one smash into a tree in revenge for taking poor Snowy.

The head witch went by the name of Zilda. Her girls, as she liked to call them, were Ogen, Ruma and Edra.

No one knew how long the witches had stalked Neverland. The Opacanta claimed they'd arrived around a hundred years ago. They'd always looked old, they never changed. Once an old hag, always an old hag. The funny thing was that everyone who came to Neverland from the outside managed to stay the same age. If you were young when you arrived, you stayed young; if you were old, you stayed old. None of this affected the Opacanta, though: they grew up, got old and eventually died quite naturally.

On this particular evening, the No-No Zone was a hive of activity. The previous night had been a great success – three bodies, the witches' best catch for months. One floating off Pirate Cove, a dead pirate who'd most likely fallen into the sea while drunk. The second body, they'd spotted floating three miles off the south of the island, a sailor from an unknown ship. The third was a member of the Opacanta tribe, who had died at a ripe old age.

Opacanta custom dictated that they clean the dead body, surround it with flowers, let it lie in peace overnight, and finally, at dawn, cremate the body.

The family of the deceased sat with the body all night, a separate fire lit nearby to keep evil spirits at bay. So when Edra and Ogen flew over they spotted the tell-tale signs of a pre-cremation fire and reported back to Zilda, who organised an attack.

Swooping low, they caused panic amongst the family, who tried to fight back, but the witches easily overcame them. The poor man's body was snatched from his resting place and carried off into the No-No Zone.

Easy pickings for the witches. Totally heart-breaking for the Opacanta.

Seeing the devastation in the morning, Migizi looked up at the sky and quietly asked, for the millionth time, 'Why can't others just leave us in peace? What harm have we ever done anyone?'

Two enormous cauldrons sat bubbling away on the beach, stirred by Edra and Ogen, while Zilda squeezed the oils from huge bunches of flowers to add to their lotions and creams. Scraps of recently dead humans' clothing lay scattered around, with crates of empty jars and bottles. Finally, Ruma, who had the best handwriting, used the quills and ink they'd stolen from the *Jolly Roger* to make labels for each jar.

Today, they were making face cream. 'Not a bad batch,' Zilda commented as she sniffed the bottle handed to her by Ogen.

Business had been good for many years, but since Hook's disappearance, there were significantly fewer dead bodies to be had.

'Things are not good, girls,' said Zilda. She lit her pipe and enjoyed a few puffs of strong dark tobacco.

'Since Hook died, well, you know what it's done to our supply of fresh corpses.'

The three others nodded in agreement.

'We can't just rely on the odd washed-up body, or the Opacanta – they never die of anything except old age. We must up our efforts – we must focus on finding the Lost Boys' hideout. Just think of those juicy young bones walking around in that jungle. And, as of tonight, we no longer have the luxury of waiting for people to die – we need to take them alive. Pirates, Opacanta, passing sailors, anyone!'

The other witches knew she was right, but even for them, killing was a big step into the unknown. Whatever the Lost Boys thought, the witches hadn't murdered anyone yet, not even poor Snowy. He was injured in the fight when they grabbed him and was therefore dead by the time they dropped him in the No-No Zone.

What Zilda now proposed didn't sit comfortably with them, especially Ruma. It was murder.

Ruma, by far the least wicked of the witches, had a bad feeling about this. It was a step too far. Of course, she'd never dare say so to Zilda.

Zilda could sense her girls' uneasiness, but warned them, 'Never forget that we're fighting for our survival here. Desperate times, girls, call for desperate measures . . .'

CHAPTER 9

It was almost dark by the time Tink returned to the hideout. The boys were making their way up the rope ladders to their beds when she swooped in like a firestorm. She buzzed around, jabbering away and not making any sense whatsoever. Finally, Obi got hold of her in his hand – never a straightforward thing to do with a fairy – and squeezed gently to make her shut up for a second.

'What's got into you, Tink? Calm down, you'll attract the witches.'

Tink was near bursting point, but Obi was right, she did need to be quiet. She held her hands up in surrender, and Obi placed her gently on a rung of the ladder.

'Boys, no one can go to bed right now, we have to talk.'

'I'm tired, Tink,' said Twin 1, quickly followed by Twin 2, 'Me too.'

Tink, in a mix of seriousness and excitement said, 'Boys, listen . . . everyone back downstairs. Take your fireflies, but only use one each.'

Once back at ground level, the boys' sleepiness soon disappeared as Tink explained about her chat with Peter. She stressed again that they were in danger of losing him.

She even told them that Peter had said he didn't want to be their leader anymore.

'I fear he's going to leave us, boys. He's falling in love with Wendy. I worry he wants to grow up and become an adult.'

Shock and panic all around. Apart from Tootles, who didn't get it.

'Hang on, whoa!' Everyone stopped talking and turned to face him. Tootles spoke directly to Tink.

'And this awful news is making you excited? You gone mad, Tink?'

'I'd tell you if you'd just let me get to the good bit!'

'Go on then.'

She paused, licking her lips and smiling a truly mischievous smile before announcing, 'I think . . . Hook is still alive!'

'What? You *have* gone mad!' The boys all started jabbering at once. Finally, when she got the chance, Tink told them about her conversations with Ilba and Migizi.

And the boys started to believe.

Discussions went on deep into the night over what to do, how to prove that Hook was still alive, how to find him. There were voices for and against action, voices of excitement, voices of caution, but the boys soon came to realise that something had to be done.

'So, what's the plan, Tink?' asked Nibs, once everyone was finally on board. 'Even if we can confirm Hook is alive, so what? What good will that do us?'

Tink looked like she meant business. The boys' eyes were full of expectation.

'There's only one thing that will bring Peter Pan to his senses . . . the return to Neverland of Captain James Hook!'

The boys were astonished, but before they could ask questions, Tink continued, 'We get everyone on board, the Opacanta, the mermaids, even the pirates. And we start a . . . a *Bring Back Hook* campaign.'

After a flurry of murmurs, the boys declared, 'You're a genius, Tink!'

Feeling extremely proud of herself, she replied, 'I know.'

'Right, boys, time for bed. We've got a lot to do tomorrow, and tomorrow will be here in a few hours. We have to plan.'

The boys climbed up the rope ladders and into their beds. Tink flew up into her little house, a large wooden box, not unlike a doll's house, which Peter had made for her. She got into bed and as she curled up in her blanket (which was really just a scrap of cloth), she said to herself, 'Hook's alive, I know it, I can feel it. This will do it – this will bring Peter Pan out of his daze, and then Wendy and London will have no hold over him. He'll soon realise where his future lies . . . in Neverland, with me and the Lost Boys.'

But then she realised the snag. She'd promised the boys a huge coordinated campaign involving the mermaids and the Opacanta. But how on earth was she going to persuade either of them to help bring Hook back to Neverland? They hated him.

'Hmm, it needs some thought, that one . . .' but she couldn't fight her tiredness a second longer.

Tink, like the boys, was soon fast asleep. It had been an exhausting day. And she extinguished her tiny glow of light just in time, as Zilda and Ogen, circling high above on their brooms, had already spotted something. But the hideout was now in total darkness and the boys were safe. For now . . .

'Have patience, my dear,' said Zilda to the frustrated Ogen, who was desperate to catch a Lost Boy and make him pay for killing one of their fellow witches. 'We'll get them, it's only a matter of time,' and with an evil laugh, off they flew.

* * *

When she woke the following morning, Tink noticed that Peter's bed had not been slept in. Again. He'd spent the night in London. Again. Normally she'd be fuming at this and in a foul mood all day, but not today, not anymore. She was focused on her plan to find Hook and save Peter from adulthood.

She still didn't know how she was going to get the mermaids on board, let alone the Opacanta. But the pirates would be easy. She'd go and meet with them, turn on the charm. She reckoned it wouldn't take much to persuade them to help. Ilba wasn't the only one in Neverland who could flirt . . .

First, though, was the problem of the Lost Boys' weight gain. Peter was right, they *were* getting podgy – and something was going to have to be done about it straight away, so that when Hook returned, they'd be in peak condition to take him on and win. Tink decided on a week-long boot camp. But first she cleared the kitchen of honey. Bread was also banned, as well as fruit. And definitely no more berry wine.

Tink explained the new regime to the boys – and to say they were not impressed would be a huge under-statement.

'When was the last time you swung on a jungle vine?' she asked them.

Nibs piped up, 'I did, last week!'

'Yeah, but it broke, and you fell into a river.'

'Shut up.'

One by one, the Lost Boys prodded their bellies . . . maybe they had put on a few pounds.

'So, what's the plan, Tink?'

'Boot camp! Tootles will be in charge.'

'What do we have to do?'

'Behave as you used to. You get up very early . . .'

Groans.

'First thing, jogging on the spot, followed by stretching, a two-mile run and a swim before returning here for breakfast.'

'Honey and bread!'

'No. We need low sugar, low carbs. Water and avocados, nothing else. Meat or fish for evening meal.'

'No honey?'

'No honey.'

'Maybe some wine in the evening? As a treat?'

'No wine either.'

More groans.

Tink reminded them of the situation they were in, and why they were doing this. Grudgingly, they agreed to the plan.

'Right, I'll leave you to it. Remember, Tootles is in charge. Listen to him and let's get fighting fit again!'

* * *

Tink had been sitting with Migizi and two of his men for a long twenty minutes. She'd been trying to enlist their help in finding Hook and bringing him back to Neverland, but it was never going to happen. As far as the Opacanta were concerned, nothing positive could come of Hook returning to Wanallah. The mere thought of it deeply concerned Migizi, although he understood Tink's reasoning.

'I won't stand in your way,' he said, 'but I can't offer any physical help to bring Hook back to Wanallah.'

Tink was disappointed, but not surprised. The Opacanta, who once had Neverland all to themselves, now shared it with the Lost Boys, who weren't actually a problem, but also witches and of course pirates who regularly shot at them on passing ships. If this wasn't bad enough, the pirates' real aim was to find and steal the gold which was rumoured to run in thin seams throughout the island, and thick seams within the inner jungle. Although, thankfully, the pirates had yet to find a way to penetrate the inner jungles. The Opacanta themselves had no particular use for gold, although they occasionally made teeth from it. But Migizi knew that if the pirates then the outside world ever discovered the extent of the gold in Wanallah, the invasion of outsiders would wreck his island for ever.

Migizi spoke again. 'And I urge caution. Have you considered this properly? Have you forgotten what Hook has done to us for years? He has killed some of your boys, and his aim is to kill Peter Pan. His pirates try to plunder our forests for their natural resources. And my people are under constant threat from him. Why would you choose to bring this pain back to us?'

'If we bring Hook back, I promise you, he'll never bother you again.'

'And how do you propose to achieve that, little Bell?'

'I don't know. But if I find him and bring him back,

I'll make him promise to leave you alone and let you live in peace.'

'That's all my people have ever wanted . . .'

Migizi was getting old, Tink could see that. The last thing she wanted was to bring him any grief. 'I'll do it, trust me.'

As Migizi watched Tink fly off, he said to himself . . . *Be careful. Be very careful what you wish for, little Bell.*

* * *

Ilba was next, and she was struggling to understand what Tink was asking of her.

'Are you serious? You want me to help being Hook back? Why should I and my sisters do such a thing? We hate Hook and his pirates.'

Tink had known that this was going to be difficult, so she'd come prepared.

'It's been rather quiet of late, wouldn't you say, Ilba? When's the last time you caught a pirate? When's the last time you found one swimming in your lagoon?'

'I can't recall . . .'

'Exactly! There's no adventure in Neverland anymore. For any of us. Don't you miss teasing and luring pirates into your water? Don't you miss chasing the *Jolly Roger*? Don't you miss sabotaging them as they hunt whales? Don't you miss those things?'

'Well . . . maybe . . .'

'Sure you do, and we can have it back, but only if we find Hook.'

She had Ilba on a hook and just needed to reel her in.

'You like Peter, don't you?'

'Yes . . .' Ilba was not sure where this was going.

'I mean you *like* him, don't you,' Tink said it with a knowing twitch of her eyebrows. A look between two females.

'He's cute, yes . . .' admitted Ilba.

'He's leaving. Leaving Neverland for good. And it's partly your fault . . .'

'My fault?'

'It was you who told him to go and find his . . . what was the word you used? Ah yes, I remember . . . *his focus,*' Tink emphasised, using her tiny fingers to make two large quotation marks. 'Well he has, he's found his focus . . . and it's Wendy. Peter is leaving Neverland and he's going to move to London, stay with Wendy and grow up. You'll never see him again. None of us will.'

'That's not what I intended.' Ilba looked shocked, and more than a bit guilty.

'That may be, but you've helped push him away – we all have, I guess. But there is a way to fix it.'

'Tell me . . .'

'There's only one way to stop Peter Pan from leaving Neverland and growing up, and that is the return of Hook. And you could help me find him . . . but then again . . . no. No, it wouldn't work . . .' Tink was playing Ilba for all she was worth.

'Why won't it work?'

'Well . . . I'm guessing you mermaids might be scared of Captain Hook . . .'

Ilba's eyes narrowed, and turned from blue to green, her face now resembling a sea snake's. When she spoke, the words came out as a hiss. 'Don't play games with me, Tinkerbell. Don't push me.'

'All right, all right,' said Tink. But her plan was working.

'So, you'll help me?'

Ilba thought carefully before replying. '. . . Yes . . . yes, we will.'

'Excellent!' cheered Tink. 'But we need to find him first.'

'Leave that to me and my sisters, we'll swim far and wide, put the word out. If Hook's on that island, we'll find him. Do you want us to approach him?'

'No, stay away, don't let him see you. Report back to me instead.'

A moment of quiet reflection passed between the two before Ilba admitted, 'You were right, Tinkerbell.'

'What?'

'It has been far too quiet round here of late. Time to bring life back to Neverland.' She winked, slipped under the water and disappeared.

Tink let out an enormous sigh of relief. Job done. So far, so good. Time to check in on the Lost Boys and see how boot camp was getting on.

* * *

Standing on an old tree stump two feet off the ground gave Tootles an air of superiority. He was the boss of boot camp after all, Tink had said so.

Earlier he'd made the boys swim and run and stretch. Now he was drilling them, army-style. He had them in single file, marching up and down through a clearing. He chanted, and the boys repeated each line in unison, parrot-fashion.

'We are going to lose the fat!'
'We are going to lose the fat!'
'Let us make no doubt of that.'
'Let us make no doubt of that.'

'We will jump and run and run.'

'We will jump and run and run.'

'Whatever it takes to get the job done.'

'Whatever it takes to get the job done.'

'Lost Boys need a brand new look.'

'Lost Boys need a brand new look.'

'To get us ready to fight old Hook!'

'To get us ready to fight old Hook!'

'Excellent!' cried Tootles. 'And again from the top!'

Tink watched from a nearby bush. 'Great, Tootles will whip the boys into shape in no time.' Suddenly, Peter appeared.

'Hey, what's going on?' he said as he landed on the ground beside Tootles.

'Eh, we, eh . . .'

We can't let him know what's going on, not yet, thought Tink, and quickly came to Tootles' rescue. 'I thought the boys were getting lazy, and they agreed, so we decided to get fit.'

'Sure they are lazy, but what's the reason for getting fit all of a sudden?'

'For health. Healthy minds, healthy bodies!' she smiled.

Peter shrugged. 'Whatever. I'm tired, I'm going to my bunk for a sleep. Can you try to keep the noise down please?'

'Sure thing,' said Tootles. 'Right, men! Grab your spears, we're going fishing.' The boys grabbed their spears and got back into single file. With Tootles at the front, they hacked their way through the jungle and the chant started again in a whisper.

'We are going to lose the fat . . .'

CHAPTER 10

The following evening, Peter once again flew to London. After supper with Mr and Mrs Darling, he and Wendy went upstairs.

Wendy sat on the end of her bed, while Peter chose the windowsill so he could gaze out over the rooftops of London. He loved the chimneys and the smoke that curled up from them.

Peter had been filling Wendy in with the latest news from Neverland. Not that there was much to tell.

'Is it true that the boys are getting fat, Peter?' Wendy found it hard to believe.

'Yes, they are. Too much honey and no playing, I guess.'

'Well, then you must whip them into shape. It's not healthy for young boys to be overweight.'

'I had a long chat with Ilba the other day,' said Peter, keen to move the conversation on.

'Oh, how is she? I like her . . . but . . .'

'She's scary?' asked Peter with a glint in his eye

Wendy nodded. 'Not scary like Hook-scary of course, but, well . . . you know what I mean.'

'Yeah, I do. Tink says . . . Tink says that if I . . .'

'If you what?'

'If I kiss her, Ilba I mean, she'll turn into a hideous catfish. Do you believe it's true?'

Wendy laughed. 'No Peter, of course not. Neverland may be a magical place, but no, I doubt Ilba will turn into a catfish if you kiss her.'

There was a long pause, then Wendy asked, 'Do you want to kiss her, Peter?'

'No . . . just asking.'

'Good,' she replied with a big smile.

'Why?'

'Well, I'd much rather you kissed me instead.'

'Why would I want to do that?' Peter felt embarrassed.

'Don't you want to kiss me, Peter? I think you do. I want to kiss you . . .'

They had kissed before, of course. But it had been more of a kiss between two good friends.

Wendy walked over to the windowsill and sat next to Peter. Their knees touched, and she took his hands in hers. Slowly she leaned in and kissed him full on the lips.

Peter kept his eyes open, looking like a startled rabbit.

Seconds later, he pulled back. 'I'm sorry, I . . . I don't know how to do it.'

'Just relax and close your eyes.'

Nervously, Peter did. He imagined the Lost Boys making faces and vomit-sounds behind his back, but he didn't care. This was nice.

Is this what Ilba meant? he thought. *Is this my new focus?*

Eventually, the kiss ended. Wendy brushed his cheek, smiled and said, 'I love you Peter Pan. But you already know that, don't you.'

If Wendy had said this to him a year ago, he'd have

flown straight out of the window, but not now.

'Yes, I think so . . . but I don't really know what love is. Is it a kiss?'

'It can be, but it's much more than a kiss. I think it's when you want to be with one person more than anyone else.'

Peter didn't reply, but he nodded his head as if he understood. Wendy sensed he was uncomfortable, so she changed the subject.

'You said you spoke with Ilba. What did she say?'

'I told her I was unhappy, and she said I had to find a new focus.'

'What does Tinkerbell have to say about this?'

'Well . . . I told her that there was nothing left for me in Neverland.'

'Really?'

'Yes, really.'

'How did she take it?'

'How do you think? Said it was all your fault. Said I'd abandoned the Lost Boys by coming here to see you.'

Knowing what Tink was like, that news came as no surprise to Wendy. She genuinely liked her. Who wouldn't love a real live talking fairy? But Wendy knew from experience how jealous Tinkerbell got when it came to Peter Pan. She asked him gently, 'Peter, what do you wish for? You can tell me, I won't tell anyone, it can be our secret.'

Peter couldn't lie to her. 'What I want is for everything to be exactly like it was before. You'll think I'm crazy, but I wish Hook wasn't dead. I just want to have adventures like before.'

'Can't you have another life in Neverland now? A different one?'

'No. It's not the same, it'll never be the same. It's just not for me anymore. Maybe I could stay here?'

'Of course you can stay tonight. Mother and Father won't mind, you know that.'

'No, Wendy, not for the night. I mean, stay here with you and your family . . . for good.'

Had he really just said that?

He had.

There was a long, awkward pause, before Wendy said quietly, 'Peter, please, don't tease me.'

'I'm not. I'm serious, Wendy.'

Wendy still didn't believe him. 'Peter, you realise we're in London. This is real life. In a few years, I'll be grown-up but you'll still be Peter Pan, the boy who never grows up.'

'Well . . . that's not entirely true,' Peter replied mischievously.

'What do you mean?'

Although he'd never mentioned it to anyone before, Peter told Wendy what Tink had explained to him many years ago.

'The magic of never growing up only stays in me if I stay in Neverland.'

'But you're not in Neverland right now.'

'I know that, silly, but I'm only here on a visit. Tink told me that if I leave Neverland and stay somewhere else, the magic of never growing up will gradually fade.'

'You mean you'd grow up? Like the rest of us?'

'I guess so. That's what Tink said.'

'But doesn't that scare you, Peter? Leaving Neverland and growing up, I mean?'

'It used to . . . but no. Not anymore. Wendy, Hook is dead and he's not coming back. And I can't change that, much as I'd like to.' Peter took a long pause before adding, 'Maybe it really *is* time for me to finally grow up.'

This was exactly what Wendy had dreamed of from the very first day she'd met him. But she was still cautious.

'But Peter, it's such a big step. Are you sure? I mean, I'd hate it if something went wrong.'

'But how could anything go wrong?'

'Peter, you just told me that you'll start to grow up. And once that happens, I guess no magic in the world could ever turn you back into a carefree boy again. If you came to live in London, there would be no going back.'

Peter looked very serious at this, and Wendy expected him to change his mind at once, realising he'd made a huge mistake. But instead he said, 'I don't want to go back. As Tink always told me when she was teaching me to fly: don't look back, you're not going that way.'

Wendy smiled, placed her hands on Peter's shoulders and told him again, 'I love you, Peter Pan.'

A long pause before Peter uttered words he'd never said to anyone in his life.

'I think . . . I think I "love" you too, Wendy.'

They kissed again. And of course, neither of them noticed a tiny light perched on the balcony railing outside the nursery window.

Tinkerbell.

She had followed Peter all the way to London. And she'd just seen and heard everything.

Her light, which usually glowed a pleasant gold colour, turned to a fiery red. She was beyond angry – she was ready to explode into a ball of flames. It took all of Tink's inner strength to stop herself from flying into the room and pulling Wendy's hair to shreds.

She couldn't stand it anymore, and her little ball of burning red light flew off into the night sky.

Wendy felt as if she could fly, too. She got up and waltzed herself round the nursery. Peter smiled – she looked so happy, she was glowing.

'Oh Peter, I can't wait to tell Mother and Father the news about you coming to stay with us!'

'Not yet,' Peter cautioned. 'There are other people to tell first.'

'You mean back in Neverland?'

'Yeah. I need to tell the boys, they deserve to know, give them time to find a new leader.'

Wendy held Peter's hands tightly. 'What will you say to Tinkerbell?'

Peter puffed out his cheeks and shook his head. 'I have no idea.'

He turned, looked out of the window and over the rooftops and chimneys of London. That was one conversation he *really didn't* want to have.

CHAPTER 11

Smee never believed that they'd spend the rest of their days on that small island. But not for a second did he believe that they could go back to Neverland – those days were well and truly over. What he did believe, though, was that eventually a ship would sail by and spot them. Then they'd get on it and take off for somewhere more civilised, to start a new life. As for where and how, Smee hadn't thought that far.

In the meantime, he just got on with life, making the best of it in his unique, cheery way. The same could not be said for Hook.

Initially, in the weeks after landing on the island, Hook was determined to make a swift comeback and return to Neverland in a blaze of glory. He'd marched back and forth along the beach with his hook swinging, plotting and scheming what he would do once he got back to Neverland.

'Damn those Opacanta for a start!' he'd say. 'I'll take all their gold, and I'll pull the gold teeth out of that senile old chief's mouth by my own hook if I have to! Then I'll take care of those annoying, interfering Lost Boys. I'm going to sell them all to the witches. Yes, that's what I'll do with them!'

'What about Pan, Cap'n?'

At the mention of Peter Pan, Hook didn't shout or get angry – quite the opposite. His voice dropped to a whisper, yet dripped with such venom it made even Smee shudder.

'What was it Pan always used to say? To die would be an awfully big adventure? Oh, Peter Pan, you are going to suffer like no boy has ever suffered before.'

Within days of being washed up on their small island, Smee had built them a hut. Then, three weeks later, having got their strength back by eating lots of fruit and fish, they'd planned their escape. They built a raft out of stripped bamboo canes – well, Hook barked orders and Smee did the building, but he didn't mind.

But it never worked. The waves were far too powerful, and they struggled to get over them and out to the open ocean. Their makeshift rafts got thrashed around, sending them flying into the water. On the only occasion they had made it past the waves, neither of them had the strength to keep rowing, and the strong ocean tides soon washed them back to shore.

It's easy to see why Hook lost all hope.

It began as a gradual slide, but had accelerated in the past six months, and now Hook was at his lowest ebb. Smee observed him, mumbling nonsense to himself. It wasn't a pleasant sight.

Smee looked across at his captain sleeping in the hammock, which was basically Hook's old coat with branches through the sleeves and tied up with jungle twine. The truth was, he did little else these days. Smee struggled to get him to come for a walk or a swim, or do anything physical. The old man believed he no longer had a reason to live. His favourite phrase was 'I have nothing left, Smee.

Nothing. I'm going to die on this damn island.'

On two occasions in the past month, Smee had found Hook walking out into the sea, intent on ending it all. The first time, the water came up to his ribs. The second time, up to his chin.

On both occasions, Smee had managed to swim out and drag him back to the shore. Hook sputtered and coughed his lungs up, but gave no thanks to Smee for once again saving his life. In fact, he got extremely angry, especially the second time.

Smee scanned the vast ocean. Where exactly they were was still a mystery to him. He knew he'd initially sailed east of Neverland, but after picking up Hook, he'd let the current take them to the sanctuary of this island. Which could be anywhere. Smee scanned the horizon yet again. No ships.

Their little island really was beautiful, and Smee was glad of the break from being a pirate – but he knew they couldn't live there forever. Even with a constant supply of fresh water, fruit and fish, it wasn't enough. Somehow, they'd have to find a way back to civilisation, before Hook lost all hope and simply faded away.

Every night Smee built a fire, sending huge flames up into the starry sky, in the hope that a passing ship would spot them . . .

CHAPTER 12

As the sun began to break through the early morning haze on Neverland, Peter was mulling over his talk with Wendy the night before. And the kissing. He was a bag of mixed emotions at the thought of leaving, and his heart felt heavy. But he regretted nothing.

His main concern was the Lost Boys. Sure, Tink had brought them to Neverland in the first place, but they were his boys. He'd taken on the role of leader and had taken care of them. He'd turned them into one big family where everyone looked out for each other. He'd given them endless amounts of fun and pleasure, and saved their individual lives countless times. The boys were his responsibility. He would not simply walk away.

Tootles, being the biggest and strongest of the boys, was the obvious choice for next leader. And of course Peter would make sure the transition was smooth. He'd make sure the boys knew of all the dangers that still existed on Neverland, and knew how to protect themselves. He'd speak with the Opacanta – they'd keep an eye on the boys after Peter was gone. As he flew high over Neverland, Peter concluded that the boys would be OK.

But then he remembered Tinkerbell.

Tinkerbell had been everything to Peter. He owed his life to her.

Peter, of course, was Neverland's original Lost Boy. When he was still only a baby in his pram, he overheard his mother telling a friend all the plans she had for his future, as they walked through Kensington Gardens. But there was no talk of a wonderful childhood – it was all about school, boarding school, university, a job in a lawyer's office, working up to his own practice and finally marriage and children of his own. Peter – who could hear and understand, though he couldn't yet speak – was horrified and started to cry. As the tears rolled down his tiny face, a small fairy passing by was so moved by the sight of the heartbroken boy that she lifted him up and carried him off to the safety of Neverland.

The boy's parents were devastated – but with the birth of another child, they soon forgot all about baby Peter. And Peter, rescued by Tink from a life of conformity and growing up, never looked back.

Tink cared for the small boy, fed him and looked after him. She taught him the ways of Neverland, and how to fly. Then, realising that Peter missed human company, she scooped up other boys who fell out of their prams in Kensington Gardens, and – if the adult looking after them didn't immediately run to pick them up – flew them back to Neverland.

Peter was forever in Tinkerbell's debt, and he knew it. That was why telling her what he now planned to do with his life was going to be devastating for her.

* * *

Back at the Lost Boys' hideout, boot camp was going remarkably well, though not without the occasional hitch.

Nibs was punished and made to do extra star jumps after being caught eating forbidden fruit, while Curly threatened to go on strike if he wasn't allowed at least one spoonful of honey. But Tink took a firm hand: when their spirits dropped, she reminded them of their goal, and they soon got their motivation back. As a result, the boys were already looking leaner, fitter and more determined.

After a morning of gruelling exercise, they ate a late breakfast of avocado soup.

'Tasty enough, but *not as good as honey*,' grumbled Curly.

After breakfast, it was time for target practice. The twins took the supplies out of a box: bows and arrows, slingshots, catapults and blowpipes.

For the next two hours, the boys took aim at a variety of fruits, placed strategically by Tinkerbell in the surrounding bushes and trees.

Everything's going to plan, Tink thought as she sat and observed them getting better and better.

'Bullseye!' shouted Tootles as Curly's arrow hit the middle of a huge ripe mango, sending chunks of fleshy fruit flying in all directions.

But Curly just sighed.

'What's up, Curls?'

'Just look at that fruit lying around, and we're not allowed to eat it!'

Tink laughed and reminded him that their sacrifices would be worth it in the end. This caused Obi to grunt and shake his head before saying quietly to himself, 'Don't see Tink doing much sacrifice.' He was convinced she'd been at the honey, but couldn't prove it.

Suddenly Tootles declared, 'OK, enough work for one day, boys. Fun time.'

'Food fight!' yelled Tink at the top of her voice. The boys didn't need to be told twice, and soon the entire area around their camp was a mess of bodies and flying chunks of fruit that exploded into juicy gunge when it hit its intended target.

As Peter slowly descended towards the ground, he took in the commotion around him.

'What's going on here?'

'Food fight!' cried the boys, as an enormous chunk of watermelon came whizzing past Peter's left ear.

'Hey, watch it. Stop messing around.'

But no one took any heed, and the fun continued. No one even noticed that Peter, who used to love nothing more than a good food fight, didn't join in the fun. Instead he stood with his arms folded, looking cross.

'Cut it out, you lot.' But again, no one took the slightest bit of notice of their leader.

As Peter stood in the middle of the chaos, Twin 1 saw his chance to play one of Peter's favourite games. In fact, it had been Peter himself who'd taught the twins how to use a blowpipe, and now they were the best shots in Neverland. Dangerous things, blowpipes, but great fun if you got it right.

When it came to pirates, the boys' favourite trick was to insert a hornet, rattle the blowpipe to make the hornet very angry, and finally, taking care not to swallow the insect, point the pipe towards a pirate and blow.

When that angry hornet hit the pirate's backside – well, you can imagine the power of the sting. The combination of blowpipe, hornet and the twins' accuracy was without a doubt one of the Lost Boys' best weapons.

Twin 1, with a cheeky grin on his face, stuffed a big, fat, juicy slugberry into his blowpipe. He blew quick and deep and out the berry shot, hitting Peter slap bang on the back of his neck. Splat!

Twin 1 put his hand over his mouth and giggled, as Peter yelped and his hand went to his neck to wipe off the splatted juice. Peter would usually cheer such a great shot, but not this time.

'Ouch! That hurt! Who did that?'

The twins couldn't stop giggling.

'I said, who did that?' He now sounded like an angry adult.

'Me, of course!' said a small voice.

'What's wrong, Peter?' asked Tink, taken aback at his reaction. 'The boys are only playing games.'

'Well, I've had enough of silly games, you're acting like a bunch of children.'

'But we are children. It's what we do,' said Twin 1 with a big, innocent smile.

As Peter turned to face the boys, his face hardened and he spat out, 'Then maybe it's time you all . . . GREW UP!'

It was if his words had physically slapped them hard, right across their little faces.

A stunned silence amongst they boys. Even Peter was surprised at his own words.

The birds in the trees fell silent. Even the insects stopped humming and buzzing.

Finally, Twin 1 burst into tears.

Tink, for once in her life, didn't know what to think or say.

Peter muttered a quick 'sorry' and flew off.

CHAPTER 13

Meanwhile, the mermaids had concentrated their efforts on the small islands surrounding Neverland. But after a week, they'd drawn a blank.

'Nothing to report,' said Ilba to Tink. 'Maybe Hook's not alive after all? It was a long shot . . .'

Tink was having none of it. 'No, Ilba, it has to be true. Remember the smoke signals from the Meshot? You need to swim further, we have to find him.'

Tink described Peter's recent outburst, telling the boys to grow up. Ilba nodded her head.

'OK Tink, we'll swim further.'

The Lost Boys were once again fighting fit. The only problem was, there was still no one to fight.

'How are we going to find Hook?' asked Zee.

'We're doing everything we can,' Tootles reminded the boys.

'It's not enough though, is it?'

'What more can we do? We can't swim like mermaids.'

'Let's take a boat out and search. We could steal a couple of small rowing boats from the pirates . . .'

'Yes, but search where? There's an entire ocean out there, thousands of miles of it. No way. We'd get lost or sunk.

We are land-based boys, the open sea is not our friend.'

Tootles was right, of course.

The boys sat in silence.

Finally, Curly said, 'What about the pirates?'

'What about them?' replied Tink.

'Well, you did say that maybe they would help us find Hook, if he's still alive . . .'

'He *is* alive,' said Tink, but she sounded more desperate than positive.

The boys looked directly at Tink, their faces pleading, longing for her to do something.

* * *

Later that day, Tink flew into Pirate Cove. Once a dangerous place, it all seemed rather subdued now. She flew low over the *Jolly Roger* and finally landed on the edge of the bow, where a for-once sober Mr Edwards was cleaning out an old trunk. He didn't seem startled or shocked to see her – he looked as miserable and lost as the Lost Boys were.

Tink spent the next twenty minutes explaining to Mr Edwards everything that had been taking place.

Of course, he was initially wary, convinced Tinkerbell was playing a trick. But she was convincing and persistent, and eventually he began to come round to the idea.

'I don't know if I believe you . . . but then again, why the heck not? What else have I got to do, other than sit and drink this stuff all day?' He motioned to yet another empty rum bottle.

'The *Jolly Roger* isn't in the best shape, as you can see, but she's still seaworthy. Half our men left Neverland a long time ago, and the others . . . well, most of them are in a worse state than me. But I know of maybe six men that might be interested in your plan. I'll go and rustle them up, and if they agree, we'll set sail. Who knows, old Hook might be alive after all . . .'

'He is,' replied Tink.

Edwards scratched his rough beard, 'But where to search? The ocean is a big place . . .'

Tink told him to make Meshot Island and its surrounding islands his focus.

'Yeah, I know it. OK . . . consider it done,' said Edwards.

Tink flew off, more confident than before, yet still worried. What more could she do? Time was running out.

As for Mr Edwards, he was true to his word. He sought out his men, and found five sober enough and willing to help. Later that night, in two small rowing boats, the pirates joined the search and set sail, heading east to Meshot Island and its surrounding waters.

Tink was determined to keep it all a secret from Peter until Hook was eventually found and back on Neverland soil – but that meant most of their efforts took place at night, when he was flying to London and back. And that meant they were drawing the attention of the witches, who hadn't failed to notice the increase in comings and goings on Neverland during the hours of darkness. They were now more convinced than ever that they would find the Lost Boys' hideout sooner or later.

'Only a matter of time, my dears,' cackled Zilda.

* * *

Peter, meanwhile, was so confused and upset after his outburst at the boys that he'd taken off to his own secret hideout on the edge of the jungle. When Tink had first brought him to Neverland, she'd thought the inner jungle far too dangerous for an infant, so she'd built him a small hut in this safe spot.

As the years passed, Peter occasionally returned and spent the odd night there, for old time's sake. But now, he chose to be there, he needed space and to clear his head.

He was frustrated with the Lost Boys for their childish behaviour, throwing fruit around – but what got to him most was his own behaviour. The way he'd spoken to the boys. He'd never done that before, and he'd certainly never uttered the words 'grow up'.

As Peter lay in his hammock in the old hut, he mulled over the past days. It would mean big changes, but he was determined to stick to his plan to leave Neverland, live with Wendy and her family, and grow up.

He decided to keep himself to himself and stay at the hide for a few more days. Then he'd muster up the courage to tell the boys and Tink of his decision.

CHAPTER 14

Going from island to island, the mermaids had been swimming for hours. But apart from where the Meshot lived, they'd seen no sign of human life on land, certainly not two white men.

They had, though, spotted Edwards and his five men in their two small boats.

'Useless,' thought Ilba as she watched them aimlessly row around the vast ocean.

Countless islands of various sizes surrounded Neverland – some quite big, but some so tiny that they were no more than a large sandbank with a solitary palm tree.

Everyone had always assumed that these islands were uninhabited, though no one really knew who or what lived there. The Opacanta and the Meshot, the only two known indigenous tribes left in that part of the world, were convinced, though, that others still existed.

As for an island of cannibals . . . well, this tale came from overheard conversations in the tavern in Pirate Cove. Pirates claimed they'd stopped by to rest on a deserted island only to be chased by terrifying savages with spears. They even claimed that one of their comrades had been captured and eaten. But no one could prove it. The pirates' stories of cannibals got more elaborate the more the rum flowed in the tavern.

There were even rumours of islands populated by wild creatures. Not tigers or leopards, but mythical beasts. The Meshot claimed that giant flying monkeys lived on Volcano Island. These were highly dangerous and, unlike their more common cousins, they were meat eaters. Even when out fishing, the Meshot men always took their spears, to ward off an attack by a troop of flying monkeys.

'Enough for one day, we'll return tomorrow to search,' said Ilba. 'Time to head back to Never . . .'

'Ilba, look,' one of her sisters interrupted. 'Over there – look!'

As the waves bobbed to and fro, a small island suddenly came into view, around two hundred feet away. On it, a makeshift hut. A sure sign of human life.

'Come,' she said, 'let's go.' And off they dived, in the island's direction.

At around fifty feet from the shore, the mermaids stopped. From this distance, even if they were spotted, they'd easily be mistaken for seals or dolphins.

Suddenly a man came out of the hut and walked towards the water's edge. A short, bald man, unshaven and bedraggled, with his hands behind his back.

'Well that's definitely not Hook,' said Ilba. 'It can't be.'

The man stood at the water's edge, head down, shoulders slumped, letting the water lap over his feet. The mermaids watched, full of curiosity. *What was this crazy old fool doing?*

He looked up and stared out, before casually walking into the ocean.

Stupid things, human beings, thought Ilba. *Why is he going swimming with his clothes on?*

Even when the water came up to the old man's waist, he still kept walking. Seconds later, it was up to his shoulders, with only his head in view.

On shore, another human appeared from a clearing and took in the scene in front of him.

'Cap'n, Cap'n, no, don't do it!' he shouted as he ran down the beach to the water's edge.

As if in a last defiant gesture to the cruel world, the man in the sea raised his arm out of the water and straight up to the sky . . . and Ilba saw it. The hook. He'd put it back on specially for his own death.

'It's Hook, it really is him!' Ilba said excitedly to her fellow sisters.

But by the time she turned back, Hook had gone under.

'He's going to drown himself. Come on, quick!' And with that, the mermaids dived under the waves.

With the strong ocean tide, the mermaids couldn't find Hook at first. Had he already been swept away? They swam and ducked and dived, but no luck. Ilba knew humans could not survive for long under water. Frantically they searched, and finally a sister saw a bloated body ten feet below her, floating aimlessly. She signalled to the others, and they dived.

The mermaids dragged the old man back to the surface. He looked dead. Were they too late?

Ilba took the limp body of the old man in her arms. She lifted his head clear of the water. His face looked nothing like Hook's, certainly not the Hook she remembered. She reached below the surface with her right hand and carefully searched, and there it was. Ilba wasn't scared of this old man, but still, the sight of the hook up close gave her the shivers.

'He's not breathing. We need to get him to the shore, quickly!'

The mermaids drove him forward to the shore, as Smee watched with bewilderment. Hook had miraculously been plucked from a watery grave and was now being brought to the shore by . . . what on earth were they? Dolphins? He couldn't make it out. What kind of mystery was this?

Not until they were twenty feet from shore did Smee realise what was happening.

'I'll be damned,' he said as he took off his bandana and wiped his brow. 'It's mermaids.'

By the time the mermaids got closer, Smee was already in the water, ready to help. But he soon stopped in his tracks as Ilba did something extraordinary.

The other mermaids had often discussed whether it was even possible. It had long been a myth passed down through mermaid folklore, but to their knowledge it had never been done – or at least they'd never seen it done. Not one mermaid alive claimed to have seen it done, apart from Ilba. Her now long-dead great-grandmother had done it. Ilba had seen it, once, many moons ago.

'But how is it possible?' the young Ilba had asked.

'Focus and believe,' her great-grandmother had told her.

With the limp body of Hook in her arms, Ilba walked towards the shore. Yes, she *walked*. The top half of her body was now above water, and still she kept walking, until the lower part of her body became visible. Ilba put her right foot followed by her left onto the sand and, still carrying Hook in her arms, strode up the beach, her long, human legs glistening in the evening sun.

Her sisters gasped in astonishment. Smee stumbled backwards and fell into the sea, totally soaking himself. Too shocked to get up, he just sat there with his mouth wide open. He'd seen many things in his time, but nothing like this. A mermaid with legs? If he hadn't seen it with his own eyes, he'd never have believed it.

As Ilba walked past him, he mouthed, 'Ilba?'

She paused and nodded.

'B-but . . .' Smee stammered.

Ilba shook her head as if to say, *don't even ask*. She continued walking until she got to dry sand, where she laid Hook gently down. His skin was pasty; he didn't look good. With no time to lose, Ilba started to perform mouth-to-mouth, pumping his chest in between breaths.

Smee got himself upright and over to where Hook lay.

'You've got to save him, Ilba. You've got to!'

'Quiet, please.' She continued to pump Hook's chest.

After what seemed like an eternity, but in reality was only a minute, Hook finally spluttered and coughed up a lungful of seawater.

'Cap'n? Cap'n? Can you see me, Cap'n?'

'Smee?' A hoarse, groggy voice asked.

'Get him fresh water.'

Smee ran up the beach to their hut and scooped up a coconut shell full of water from his home-made rain barrel.

Ilba held the back of Hook's head as she studied the old man. It was hard to believe it was him.

Hook, his eyes still blurry, looked up at the woman staring back at him. The most beautiful woman he'd ever seen. *Am I dreaming?* he wondered.

Trying to focus, Hook weakly held up his hand to the woman and said, 'Mother? Is it you, Mother? Have you come back for me?'

That image soon vanished as Smee returned and brought the coconut shell to Hook's lips. He drank, licked his lips and laid his head back on the sand.

Suddenly, Ilba felt dizzy. She was drying out.

'I must get back into the water,' she told Smee. She walked unsteadily to the water's edge, slipped under and started to rehydrate. Her sisters held her up and comforted her. She was exhausted.

After giving her a few moments, the sisters bombarded her with questions.

'You did it Ilba, but how is it possible?'

'What's it like to have legs?'

'Did you feel human?'

'What's it like to walk on land?'

'Strange . . . like having an out-of-body experience. I was not me anymore, but someone else.'

Ilba looked pale, and her fellow sisters were worried she'd caught some terrible land-based human disease. But Ilba explained this was the downside of being out-of-body. It totally drained your energy. Great-grandmother had, indeed, warned her about this, and added a further warning that if she did ever manage to go out-of-body, she must do it only in exceptional circumstances, and for as short a time as possible, as if she went too far from the sea she could get stranded, then dry out and die.

'What now, Ilba?' asked a sister.

'We stay. Wait for Hook to come round. Then we take it from there.'

Back up on the beach, Hook had indeed come round. Smee had helped him back to the shade of their hut and sat him down. He gave him more water.

'What happened to me, Smee? All I can remember is everything going dark, then black. I wasn't in pain, Smee, just slipping away.' He took another drink of water.

'But I was pulled back by . . . by a woman, a beautiful woman. And I saw my mother. Or maybe not . . . did I dream it?'

Smee explained about the mermaids, and finally Ilba, who had miraculously carried him to safety.

Hook was having a tough time understanding what he was hearing.

'But it's true, Cap'n, I saw it with my own eyes. Ilba walks . . . on land.'

Hook looked at the sea and saw a clutch of mermaids bobbing in the water. It made no sense. Why would they come here and save his life? They were no friends of his. And as for Ilba somehow sprouting legs and walking – how was that even possible?

'What's going on, Smee?' asked Hook, genuinely confused.

'I don't know, Cap'n. But shall we find out?' He motioned towards the shoreline.

Hook stood up, ignoring Smee's offer of a helping hand, and walked to the edge of the beach. Ilba and the mermaids swam closer.

Speaking with none of his usual bluster, Hook said cautiously, 'I suppose I should offer you my thanks . . .'

'That's up to you, Hook,' replied Ilba.

'Then I say . . . thank you.'

Ilba nodded.

'But why? Why did you save me? In fact, why are you even here?' It made little sense to Hook - he'd lost at least a dozen men to mermaids over the years. They were sworn enemies.

'I have much to tell you, Hook. Sit down, this may take some time.'

'Smee, get me something to sit on.' He sounded more like his old self again.

Smee rushed off, picked up an old crate he'd salvaged from the sea months ago and brought it to his captain. Hook sat, while Ilba lay in the surf as close to the shore as possible. Again she was shocked at the sight of the once-proud man in front of her.

Fat belly, no teeth, completely bald.

Usually paranoid about letting anyone see him this way, Hook couldn't care less how he looked to Ilba. He simply wanted an explanation.

* * *

Back on Neverland, Migizi, the Opacanta chief, was deeply worried.

'What troubles you, wise one?' asked one of his men, sat opposite him outside his hut.

'The past . . .'

'But how can the past be something that worries you? You always told us to not focus on the past, or the future, only the present.'

'The past . . . is soon to become the present and the future.'

Migizi sensed his young warrior's confusion. He leaned forward and picked up a stick lying nearby. In the sand, he drew a large shape.

'But how is it possible?' the young man stammered.

Migizi as ever remained calm and replied, 'Anything is possible.' He returned his stare to the sea, that worried expression once again spreading across his face, while the young warrior stared in horror at the shape of a hook in the sand.

As Migizi sat contemplating, his head got tighter and tighter. He gently rubbed his temples.

So, the Meshot were right. Hook is alive. I know it. I can feel it. And soon he will return to Wanallah.

'Why can't everyone leave my people in peace?' he asked the sea.

The normally unemotional Opacanta chief's chest heaved and tears started to flow down his old, lined face.

* * *

Ilba began at the beginning and explained to Hook everything that had happened since the croc incident. She described the mood on the island since he'd been gone, and explained about the Meshot, the Opacanta and Tink's 'Bring Back Hook' campaign. Hook sat in silence until she'd finished.

'So, everyone wants old Hook to return to Neverland?'

'Well, not exactly everyone . . .'

'And what about you? What do you want, Ilba?'

'It's not for me to say. I'm merely fulfilling a promise to Tinkerbell.'

Ah yes, little Tinkerbell. He'd never forget that one.

She'd caused him much trouble over the years. Oh, how he'd like to wring her tiny neck.

Hook contemplated everything Ilba told him. Then it suddenly dawned on him.

'How can I return to Neverland? Look at the state of me. My hair, my teeth, I can't . . .'

'We can help with that.'

'How?'

'Just wait. However, right now we must leave, but we will return . . .'

'No! Don't you dare leave me here. I can't take it anymore . . .'

Ilba momentarily felt sorry for him. He was weak – pitiful, even. Could he ever be the same again? Was it even worth bringing him back to Neverland? But that wasn't her decision to make.

'Hook, I made a promise to Tinkerbell. I will be back. Meantime, you've got to get yourself together. We can help with the hair and teeth, but you must get this together,' she said, pointing at his head.

'We'll be back in a week, to do what we can.' And with that, she disappeared under the water.

'A remarkable creature . . . woman . . . fish . . . whatever she is,' said Hook.

'What now, Cap'n?'

'What now, you ask, Smee? Our fightback starts today, that's what. No more lounging around for you, Smee. No more sitting about getting fat and wallowing in self-pity. We will exercise, we will walk and swim and get our strength back. Come, we'll start now!' And with that Hook marched along the beach.

'C'mon Smee,' he called back over his shoulder. 'Get

those legs moving! And bring the spears, we're going fishing!'

Smee picked up two spears and happily trotted after his captain. Back in control, barking orders and full of confidence. The captain he loved.

'Praise those mermaids,' he said to the sky as he caught up with Hook.

CHAPTER 15

Over the next week, the mermaids were busy. Very busy indeed.

They crafted a set of gleaming white false teeth from mother-of-pearl shells, and even managed to come up with a new wig, painstakingly hand-made from dried seaweed, which they covered with the hair of wild pigs then dyed with blackberries. It looked surprisingly good.

But the clothes proved to be more of a challenge. Although not able to kit Hook out to his usual standards, Tink did the best she could under the circumstances.

On three sneaky trips into Pirate Cove, she managed to steal shoes from a sleeping pirate, right off his feet. And thanks to Slightly, a long coat, shirt and breeches had mysteriously disappeared from the pirates' washing line.

Smee had also been busy. He'd shaved his captain using mashed-up coconut pulp as a cream and the edge of a very sharp razor clam for a blade. It worked a treat. Hook was once again clean-shaven, apart from a thin moustache.

With a piece of cloth ripped from his own tatty shirt, Smee used coconut milk to polish up the hook. After a morning of hard graft it was restored to its former glory, gleaming and sparkling in the sunlight.

As for Hook, he had kept his word and exercised every day. He started early in the morning with a swim before walking the beach for an hour. In the afternoon he caught fish.

In the early evening he swam once more before it got dark. As for his mind, it got sharper by the day, and although he didn't physically look like the old Hook, he sounded more like him with every passing hour.

Smee was impressed by the humble coconut. Over the last year, it had literally been a life saver. One could drink the sweet water, eat the flesh, use the husk as a cup and carve pieces of it to make spears. And of course its sweet water also soothed sunburn and now the mashed-up pulp had been used for shaving. A most versatile fruit indeed. That said, he was sick to the back teeth of eating the damn things. If Smee ever got off the island, he vowed never to eat another coconut again. Ever.

Hook feared the mermaids wouldn't return to help save him, so he was greatly relieved when they arrived early one evening, pushing a small rowing boat. Smee ran down to the shoreline and dragged the boat up onto the sand. Inside was a parcel of clothes, and an assortment of other things, including a needle and thread, tied up in a protective wrapping of banana leaves to keep it all dry. Smee thanked Ilba and took the parcels back to the hut.

* * *

Being a dab hand with a needle and thread, Smee had made a few minor adjustments, and Hook, now fully clothed in his new attire, stepped out of the hut.

'What do you think?' he said as he walked to the shoreline.

He wasn't exactly in his prime but it was no doubt a vast improvement. Ilba considered not paying him a compliment, but in the end said, 'Not bad, Hook, not bad at all.'

That was good enough for him and he revelled in the praise.

'So, what happens next? When am I to get off this prison of an island and back to civilisation?'

'We leave now, in this boat.'

Smee voiced his concern that he didn't have the strength to row them all the way back to Neverland.

'I know,' replied Ilba, 'but we will guide you. My sisters and I will help push you.'

Smee smiled and stepped into the small boat. He offered his hand and helped Hook on board.

As far as Hook was concerned, he really was being released from prison. He turned back to face the island for the last time. He said nothing, only stared at it.

Then, turning back to face the front of the boat he declared, 'Right, mermaids, let's get a move on. To Neverland we go!'

'I give the orders around here, Hook,' warned Ilba.

Hook fought back anger. How dare anyone speak to him like that, especially a damn fish! But he knew he needed the mermaids, so wisely kept quiet.

'My apologies, Ilba.' Hook bowed his head. 'In your own time . . .'

Ilba nodded. 'You'd better sit and get comfortable, it's going to be a long ride.'

'When will we reach Neverland?' asked Hook, trying to sound as nice as possible.

'Not until tomorrow morning. You have a long night ahead.' Then added, 'And it will be an even longer night for us. I hope you appreciate what we're doing here, Hook.'

He smiled his least nasty smile, put his hand over his heart and said, 'I will be forever in your debt, my dear.'

'Right, my sisters, let's go.' And off they moved.

Hook sat beside Smee, who covered him in a blanket. The night was clear and the sky full of stars. For once, Hook didn't speak, grumble or complain. He could still hardly believe what was happening.

He sat in quiet contemplation as the small boat skipped through the water.

Eventually Hook and Smee fell fast asleep, but there was no rest for the mermaids, who continued pushing and guiding the boat towards Neverland all night, without rest or complaint.

* * *

Hook had been awake for an hour already. With the sun not yet up, it was misty, damp and cold. Really cold. None of this concerned Hook though, who was so full of adrenaline he didn't feel it.

He glanced over the side of the boat and saw the mermaids still tirelessly going about their business. *Marvellous creatures*, he thought. *Maybe I'll take one as a pet, keep it in a water tank on the* Jolly Roger? *Yes, I'd like that.*

Suddenly, the sea mist broke, the sun filtered through the haze, and within a minute the sky turned blue. The bluest sky he'd ever seen.

He heard birds and, as any pirate knows, that's a sure sign that land is not far away. Moments later, the unmistakable outline of Neverland came into view – and what a spectacular sight it was. It filled Hook's heart with joy.

He tugged on Smee's shoulder to rouse him. 'Smee . . . Smee . . . wake up, man!' Smee yawned and came to, just as Hook stood upright in the boat. Pointing straight ahead, and sounding like an excited schoolboy, he said, 'Look Smee . . . Neverland! We're back Smee, we're home!'

He breathed in the sweet air, held his hook up high in triumph and proclaimed, 'Hook is back! Onward mermaids, onward!'

Although certainly not happy at being dictated to by a pirate, the mermaids were far too tired to challenge him.

They kept going, their only wish being that this journey would soon be over.

CHAPTER 16

Sitting with the Lost Boys around their kitchen table, Tink was holding court.

'Boys, we need a council. We need to agree rules. We must get Hook on side.'

There was grumbling from the Lost Boys – all of a sudden, they were not so sure about this. Would Hook try to kill them as soon as he saw them?

'Boys, listen, we must do this. Remember – we've achieved what we wanted. Hook is alive, and he's coming back. And you know what that means? That's right – Peter Pan will snap out of it, he'll stop going to London, he won't grow up, and everything will get back to normal.'

The boys were still not convinced.

'Look, the mermaids have already told Hook why they're rescuing him. Ilba says he's grateful – humbled, even.'

Both the twins snorted at this, while Zee shook his head. Tink kept at them.

'Come on, boys, we've got to make this work. We've got to make Hook feel welcome.'

'Welcome? I thought we wanted to fight him again, not be best friends,' said Nibs.

'Yes, welcome. But it won't be for long. Look, we sit as a council and agree a truce until Peter returns from London. Then, and only then, do we start again. Think about it, boys: Peter will soon be back, Hook will be back, and it will soon be us against him, like it used to be. But in the meantime, we have to make Hook welcome, we must convince him to stay, because if he leaves, then Peter leaves . . .'

'Agreed!' they shouted in unison.

'Excellent. Right boys, let's prepare a meal, to celebrate Hook and Peter's return. No, not a meal . . . a feast. The best feast we've ever had.'

The boys liked the sound of that.

'Divide up the work between you. Tootles, I'm leaving you in charge.'

'What about you, Tink?'

'I'm going to meet Hook.'

'Be careful, Tink. Remember, he's still Hook . . .'

'I'll be careful. Now make sure this table is groaning with food when I return. Make me proud!' And off she flew.

'Wish I could fly,' said Nibs, watching Tink take off.

'Forget that. We have work to do, so get your finger out,' said Tootles, 'And go and pick some fruit.'

'Who made you leader?'

Tootles puffed out his chest. 'Tink, remember – she said I was to be in charge.'

And Tootles did indeed take charge: he made a list, gave his orders, divided up the tasks and quickly set the boys to work.

* * *

The mermaids wearily drove the small boat containing Hook and Smee into Mermaid Lagoon. It had been a long night for them.

Smee jumped out and pulled the boat up onto the sand. Hook stepped off, and after a very long year, planted his feet firmly back on Neverland soil.

After enjoying a moment to take in his surroundings, Hook turned back to the sea. 'Thank you, Ilba. You and your sisters have done a marvellous job. I salute you.'

Ilba accepted the compliment with the customary nod of her head. 'We've done our bit, Hook, the rest is up to you and Tinkerbell.'

It then dawned on Hook that he had no idea what lay ahead. Would Peter Pan appear? Would they fight straight away? Why had they not gone directly to Pirate Cove? Where were his men? And what of the *Jolly Roger*?

Ilba could sense his concern. 'I was told to bring you here,' she said. 'Now you must walk in that direction and into the outer jungle. When you come to the first small clearing, you will see a broken tree. You are to wait there.'

'For what? For whom?'

'I don't know, Hook.' She turned to her sisters. 'Come, we must rest.' They slipped under the water and vanished.

Ilba's last waking thoughts were full of doubt. Had she done the right thing? Only time would tell, she concluded, before falling into a deep, watery sleep.

After thirty minutes of walking through the forest in the direction that Ilba had pointed out, Hook too had doubts. What if he and Smee were walking straight into a trap? Were they about to be ambushed by Peter Pan and a horde of horrible Lost Boys?

But soon they came to a clearing, and there it was: a large broken branch, which had been left by Tootles and Slightly the day before.

Hook sat down and wondered if Peter Pan's hideout was nearby. But he soon dismissed the idea. There was no way they'd have agreed to meet him anywhere near that. After all, the pirates had spent years trying to find its whereabouts – he'd lost countless men in the jungle searching for it, and even made a deal with the witches, but with no luck.

Hook swished a hand over his face. 'Damn pesky mosquitoes,' he remarked. But it came back at him again and again. Hook stood up and finally shook it off. Yet it kept hovering, an arm or hook's length away. And now it was glowing.

Tinkerbell flew over to a nearby branch and, making sure she was safely out of reach, turned herself into full fairy form.

'Oh!' said Smee, pointing with delight. 'Look, Cap'n!'

Hook kept his emotions intact and drawled a sarcastic welcome.

'Well, well, well, if it isn't little Miss Stinkerbell.'

Tink stood, hands on her hips, and just snorted at him. 'Very funny, Hook. So, it's true . . . you are alive.'

'Very much so, Miss Bell.'

'Hello Tinkerbell, you look lovely,' said Smee, like a child at Christmas.

'Shut up, Smee,' said Hook.

'I see you're as charming as ever, Hook.'

Hook ignored the comment. 'I believe, Miss Bell, that I have you to thank for bringing me back here. What a turnaround, eh?'

'Yeah . . . but these have not been normal times.'

'Quite. So, what happens now? And where is Peter Pan?' asked Hook, looking nervously all around him.

'Pan's not here right now, so you'll have to deal with me. And first, a council. We need to agree rules.'

'Rules of war, you mean?'

'If you like, but before even that, we must agree a truce. An immediate truce for forty-eight hours.'

'Not trying to trick old Hook by any chance?'

'No. No tricks, just a truce, so we can establish what's what, and lay the ground rules before, well, you know . . .'

Hook wasn't sure where this was going, but decided to play along. 'Agreed.'

As soon as Tink had Hook's agreement to the truce, she called over her shoulder, 'Boys? It's safe. You can come out now.'

The faces of the Lost Boys appeared cautiously from behind trees, bushes and grass. But they were still reluctant to come forward.

'Come on,' Tinkerbell repeated. 'It's safe. We've agreed a truce, and we're going to have a war council.'

The boys, carrying spears by their sides, edged forward. Twin 2, the smaller of the pair, kept behind Tootles for protection.

Hook nodded his head in acknowledgment of the boys' presence. Tootles did likewise and, never once taking their eyes off Hook, they carefully sat in a circle on the grass, and the discussions began.

They sat in conference for most of the afternoon, each side stating their case and their demands.

'No more stealing raids into Pirate Cove or boarding the *Jolly Roger*,' demanded Hook.

Tink looked at the boys, who nodded.

She turned back to Hook and confirmed, 'Agreed,' before adding, 'No more doing deals with the witches to find our hideout.'

'Agreed,' said Hook.

'And no more whale hunting, or Ilba will sink the *Jolly Roger*.'

Hook smiled. 'Agreed. But no more of Pan bringing outsiders here from London, especially a certain young lady by the name of Wendy.'

'Agreed!' shouted Tink.

Sitting and talking with the enemy was not what Hook had expected on his return to Neverland, but after the mental torture of a year on that tiny island, he was rather enjoying communicating and making deals.

Just when he thought the negotiations were over, Tink said, 'Oh, and one more thing, Hook. The Opacanta are off-limits.'

'Why?'

'If it weren't for them, you'd still be stuck on that island. They read the smoke signals, they helped make it happen. And I made them a promise. Leave them alone, Hook. Let them live in peace.'

'And if I don't?'

'Well, I'll see to it that Ilba drags you all the way back to that tiny island and you'll be there forever.'

Hook did not like the sound of that. 'You don't ask for much, do you?'

'The Opacanta are non-negotiable, Hook.'

Hook had absolutely no intention of leaving the Opacanta alone, but he'd go along with it for now. Right now, he'd agree to anything to be able to face Peter Pan again.

'I agree,' he said. 'I won't lay a finger on them.'

But Tink needed more clarification than that. 'You won't lay a finger . . . or hook on them.'

Hook smiled a knowing smile. 'Very clever, Miss Bell. Agreed.'

'And you still agree to a forty-eight-hour truce?'

'Yes, I do.'

'OK. Now shake on it.'

Tink put out a tiny hand towards him and he replied by putting forward his gleaming silver hook. It was the first time the boys had seen it since his return, and they all edged back. Hook observed their reaction and liked what he saw. Of course they were still terrified of the hook, and rightly so. But he calmed their fears, saying, 'Boys, boys, don't worry, remember we have a truce . . .'

The gleaming, menacing hook was over three times the size of Tinkerbell's entire body, but she placed her tiny hand on it, shivering as she touched the ice-cold metal, and they shook.

Rules agreed. Deal done. Both sides were happy.

'So, what now?'

'Now?' said Tootles. 'Easy – now we eat, that's what! We've been living on avocado soup for ages. But tonight it's wild pig and berry wine for us. Old adversaries around the table, we celebrate the future, and everything being back the way it used to be!'

Hook liked the sound of this. He was sick of fish. As for Smee, he just prayed there wouldn't be any coconuts. The boys cheered, and Hook bellowed, 'Bravo! Bravo!'

'Will my old adversary Pan be joining us tonight, Miss Bell?'

'No. I told you, he's not here, he'll be in London with that Wendy, no doubt.'

Hook could see her displeasure, which he duly noted and decided he'd use to his own advantage when the time came.

'But fear not, Hook. Pan will return early tomorrow morning as he always does, and when he realises you're back in Neverland, well . . . everything will be back to normal, like we both want, yes?'

'I couldn't agree more, Miss Bell.'

'Right, come on, no more talking. Let's get everything organised and let's eat!' said an impatient Tootles, whose stomach was grumbling.

* * *

Of course, they didn't take Hook back to their hideout – they made camp where they were. Tink flew back and collected the prepared food from the hideout while the boys hastily crafted a table out of logs lashed together with vines. A fire was built, and the table soon groaned with goodies.

The freshest forest fruits filled numerous bowls, while rainbow trout caught that very morning and fried crispy were piled high. And in the middle sat a whole roasted wild pig with a huge apple stuffed in its mouth. A feast indeed.

With their wooden goblets filled with home-made berry wine, they tucked in. They gorged themselves.

It was fun and friendly, with old rivalries apparently forgotten as they shared stories from past adventures.

'He ain't so bad after all,' said Tootles to Nibs, through yet another mouthful of succulent, crispy wild pig.

'Hmm, I wouldn't trust him as far as I could throw him,' replied Nibs, never taking his eyes off Hook. 'Remember who he is, Tootles. He's Hook: don't forget that.'

Nibs rubbed gently at his right upper arm. The wound there had healed long ago, but the scar it had left, he'd have for life. Nibs had been lucky – if Slightly hadn't shouted out a warning and he hadn't spun round in time, it would have been his neck that was slashed by the hook, not his arm. Nibs rubbed his scar one last time. This jolly, friendly act of Hook's did not convince him. Not one bit.

As darkness descended over Neverland, and with stomachs full of food and wine, tiredness inevitably set in. It had been a long day for all of them.

'It's late. I won't be able to find my way to Pirate Cove in this darkness. Where am I supposed to sleep?' asked a concerned Hook.

'Right here, under the stars,' replied Tink.

Hook glanced round at Neverland's jungle. What manner of creepy-crawly things lived nearby? He shuddered to think. Suddenly, he felt decidedly uneasy. He was a ship man, and always slept on the *Jolly Roger*, be it in port or out at sea. That said, he had managed to spend the last year sleeping on a desert island. Oh, hang it, he'd survive one more night before he got back into the luxury of a proper bed aboard ship. He downed the last half-cup of berry wine and announced, 'Sleep under the stars, and why not!'

Everyone cheered. *Good stuff, this berry wine*, Hook thought.

The Lost Boys bedded down with their blankets. One twin even offered his blanket to Hook, saying he'd share with his brother.

'Why thank you, young man,' replied Hook, surprised at the genuine kindness.

'Night, Hookie,' said the sleepy, half-drunk boys.

'Night, dear boys,' replied Hook.

'Goodnight, Neverland!' crowed the boys in unison, before releasing their fireflies and plunging the camp into darkness.

It didn't take long before the boys were fast asleep. There really is only so much berry wine a boy can drink, you know.

Hook lay in silence, looking up at the starry sky. He was back, back where he belonged. He inhaled and exhaled deeply as the Lost Boys snored contentedly only feet away.

'Such charming boys, Smee,' Hook remarked innocently.

'Sure are, Cap'n, sure are.'

'And how I will enjoy making them walk the plank, before finishing off Peter Pan once and for all.'

Smee smiled. His captain was back, that was for sure. 'Goodnight, Cap'n.'

'Good night, my faithful Smee.' Hook finally closed his eyes and within minutes fell into a deep sleep. The first proper sleep he'd had in a year. No nightmares of crocodiles tonight, only dreamless, blissful sleep.

CHAPTER 17

'Oh my head . . .' Tootles sat up and rubbed his temples.

'I told you not to drink so much berry wine,' said Slightly.

'Was good, though,' replied Tootles as he managed a half smile.

'And that roasted piggy!' said Curly.

The boys agreed. The meal had been a triumph. Slightly looked over at Hook and Smee, who were still fast asleep, snoring deeply.

Hook was indeed back. A new day, a new dawn for Neverland, just like the old days.

Suddenly Tink appeared.

'Get up boys, we've got a problem.'

'What's up, Tink?'

'It's Peter.'

'Is he OK? Has he had an accident?'

'No. Much worse than that.'

'What do you mean, Tink?'

'Earlier, I flew to the hideout to give him the good news about Hook's return, but he was nowhere to be seen. And his bed hadn't been slept in either.'

'Maybe he's not back from London yet.'

If only, thought Tink. 'No, it's not that . . .'

'Maybe he spent the night in London?'

'No. Boys, listen. I've got news, and it's not good.'

The boys were fully awake now, their hangovers suddenly forgotten.

'Pan came back during the night. He left a note on his bed. I'll read it to you.'

'But Peter can't write,' said Tootles, somewhat surprised.

'I know. But just listen,' replied Tink.

Dear Tink and boys,

As you know, I can't write, so Migizi kindly wrote this letter for me. But they are all my own words.

Things are not the same in Neverland anymore. With Hook dead and gone, I see no point in staying here any longer.

I have tried to adapt, but I just can't. And I've also changed as a person. I've been visiting Wendy a lot recently and it's made me think about my future.

I'm sorry boys, really sorry, but after I drop this letter off I'm flying to London for good. I'm not coming back. I've decided to stay and take my chances with growing up. And I think it's time you all did the same.

I did want to tell you in person, but you weren't here. I guess Tink took you out on a night hunting trip. So I'm leaving this note instead.

I'm sorry, but you have the right to know.

Take care, my dear boys, and keep safe.

I will always love you.

Peter Pan.

Bombshell.

Stunned silence.

Total shock.

The boys turned ghostly white.

It can't be true . . . it just can't be true. But despite the shock, deep inside, they knew it was. Especially Tink.

They had left their plan too late. So near, yet so far.

The twins began to cry.

The boys looked directly at Tink, their faces pleading for a glimmer of hope. Although angry at Pan and especially Wendy, Tink's heart was breaking.

'It's over, boys. Peter has left. He has left us and he's not coming back.'

After what seemed like an eternity, Tootles finally asked, 'What now, Tink?'

Tink looked over at the still sleeping Hook.

'I guess I'll need to tell him . . .'

Part Two

CHAPTER 18

Three months had passed since Peter had left Neverland and as each day went by, he was getting more used to London life. It wasn't so much difficult, but it was very different.

He adored the loving, warm feeling in the Darling family home. Mrs Darling doted on him and treated him as one of her own children. She was the mother he'd never had and had always secretly longed for.

His manners though, especially at the start, left a lot to be desired. It was pointed out to Peter by everyone around the table that eating with your fingers was never acceptable. He'd used a wooden spoon back in Neverland, and of course his dagger to cut into large chunks of meat, but he'd never used knives and forks before – well, not in a proper English manner. Then there were spoons. Spoons for tea, spoons for sugar, spoons for soup, spoons for dessert, so many spoons. So much to learn.

For breakfast, Peter enjoyed his toast and marmalade. But he didn't like the porridge. For supper he liked most things, but thought cheese was horrible. 'All cheese is horrible,' he claimed.

The food on Sundays soon became his favourite – always a big piece of succulent meat, which he learned was called a Sunday roast. As Mr Darling carved, Peter would drool at the mouth. He remembered when he and the Lost Boys used to hunt and kill a wild pig and roast it whole on an open fire. He wanted to dive in, tear off an enormous chunk of meat and eat it with his bare hands. But that would simply not do. As Mr Darling kept carving, Peter forced himself to sit on his hands to keep them under control.

Wendy couldn't help but notice and always had to stifle a giggle.

By far the worst thing about his new life was bath night. Compared to bath night, learning table manners was nothing. Nana knew Sunday equalled bath night, and she stuck rigidly to the rules. Wendy, of course, didn't need to be told – she had a bath every day. But Peter, well, it was a struggle to just get him in the tub.

'What's the point of washing? I'll only get dirty again,' he protested to Nana. But she was having none of it and pulled him gently by the hair to the bathroom. To Nana, all children in the house, irrespective of their age, were like puppies. Her puppies.

Peter would stand in the bathroom with his hands defiantly on his hips, refusing to get into the tub. Nana would bark again and again, and Peter somehow knew exactly what she was saying.

Get into that bath and wash, or I'll drop you in there myself.

'All right Nana, you win, I'm getting in, I'm getting in!' Once he'd climbed into the bath, Nana would give a woof of achievement and leave him to it.

Although Peter would never admit it to anyone, once he was in the tub and soaking in the hot, foamy water, he rather enjoyed his bath night.

When Peter had arrived, his hair was a sandy-brown mop. A beautiful mop, but still a mop. A mop that needed trimming. But when Mrs Darling came to him one afternoon with a giant pair of scissors, Peter ran off and hid under his bed. He'd never seen such a wicked-looking instrument.

In the end, Mrs Darling managed to trim his hair, although not too much, and Peter even liked the result. He even enjoyed looking at himself in the mirror, once he'd got over the fear that someone else was hiding behind the frame.

Mr Darling took him to his tailor, who kitted Peter out with two sets of proper clothes. Peter liked the trousers. He didn't mind the waistcoat, or suit jacket, but he hated wearing a shirt and tie. Scratchy and choking, he complained. He loved his new stripy blue pyjamas, though.

As for shoes – well, after having had more than his fair share of stubbed toes in Neverland over the years, shoes were the best.

All in all, with his hair trimmed and combed, his new clothes on, and scrubbed after a weekly bath, Peter soon resembled just another ordinary boy.

And it wasn't only his appearance that changed, but his height as well.

'I believe you've grown, young Peter,' Mrs Darling announced one morning with a smile.

He had. He had grown an inch or two. Peter was growing up. And with each passing day, he became less and less like Peter Pan.

Then it was time to teach him how to behave outside the house.

'Remember, Peter, when you meet a lady in the street, you must tip your hat,' said Mr Darling.

'Why?'

'Because it's good manners, my boy.' Peter watched as Mr Darling and Wendy did something we today call a role play. 'Now you try, Peter.' He did, and it wasn't so bad.

'Now how would you address a lady in the street, after you tip your hat?'

Peter thought for a moment. 'G'morning missus!'

Shock and shaking of the heads followed. 'No, no, Peter, that won't do. Allow me to show you how it's done.'

Mr Darling walked towards Wendy. He stopped, bowed, tipped his hat, and said, 'And a very good day to you, Mrs White. What a fine morning it is. I wish you a pleasant day.'

'Now you try, Peter.'

'Good morning, Mrs White . . . but I don't know anyone called Mrs White,' he protested.

'It's only a game, Peter, for practice. Try to imagine you know her.'

Peter scratched his head and looked confused, but he persevered.

'Good morning, Mrs White . . .' he paused, then turned to Mr Darling and said, 'but I can't say what a fine morning it is.'

'Whyever not?'

'Because it's raining!'

'I can see this is going to take time,' Mr Darling commented wryly to his daughter.

Wendy had been teaching Peter to read and write, and he was surprisingly keen to learn. He even expressed a wish to go to school the following year, which amazed everyone in the household.

Peter had good days and bad days. To begin with, he

suffered daytime flashbacks. Of Neverland. He pictured the boys, wandering through the forests and jungles, looking for him, calling out for him. He pictured sad mermaids. But the worst thing was the nightmares, especially during his first two weeks. He dreamed of chaos; he dreamed of Neverland burning in flames.

He'd wake up in sweats. He sometimes screamed, sometimes cried. Mrs Darling comforted him, telling him the nightmares would pass with time – and she was right, they did. Whenever Peter got depressed and missed Neverland, feeling guilty about leaving, Wendy sat with him late into the night to talk. And when she wasn't at school, she tried to fill his life with as many good things as possible.

'You've shown me Neverland and all its wonders. Well, now it's time for me to show you my city.'

Trafalgar Square, Big Ben, the Houses of Parliament, Buckingham Palace – they all took his breath away. Peter couldn't believe how big everything was. He used to think that the Lost Boys' hideout with its rope bridges and huts high in the trees was impressive, but London was something else.

How had they managed to build them all? he wondered to himself.

'If you think that's impressive, wait until you read my encyclopedia.'

'A what?'

'A book, Peter, an enormous book, called an encyclopedia. It tells you all about amazing inventions all over the world.'

This book, especially because of its pictures, soon became Peter's favourite. He fell in love with the pyramids of Egypt and stories of ancient civilisations.

On weekends, they liked to walk in the parks: St James's Park, round the Serpentine in Hyde Park – and his favourite, Kensington Gardens. He always felt a particular pull towards that one.

But the best thing of all? A stall in Kensington Gardens that sold the most wonderful food he had ever tasted in his entire life.

'Try this, Peter.' Wendy handed him a cone. Peter looked at the strange white mountain on top of the thing he was holding. 'What is it?'

'Ice cream.'

Peter went to take a huge bite.

'No Peter, don't eat it like you're chewing meat. Lick it and let it melt on your tongue.' After watching Wendy demonstrate, Peter licked his first ever ice cream.

The look of surprise on his face said it all. 'I love it, Wendy! Can we eat ice cream every day?'

Covent Garden disappointed him. 'Don't you like it, Peter?' asked Wendy as she showed him around the bustling market.

'Yes, but . . .'

'But what?'

'Where's the garden?'

Wendy laughed. 'Oh Peter, there's no garden, only a market.'

'Then why do they call it a garden?'

'I really don't know,' replied a confused Wendy.

He found the museums and art galleries awfully boring, and did not enjoy his visit to the zoo.

'It's wrong, Wendy,' he said, watching a large tiger as it paced back and forth behind the bars of its cage, and Wendy could see the sadness in Peter's eyes, especially when he saw the caged birds. They didn't go back to the zoo.

* * *

On three mornings a week, Peter had a private tutor who came to the house, and the rest of the time, he liked to run errands for Mrs Darling, to the butchers and the bakers – and to Covent Garden to buy flowers.

But his favourite task was collecting and returning books to the library. His reading was improving all the time, and he marvelled at the rows and rows of books that seemed to go on forever.

One day, Peter even paid a visit to where Mr Darling worked, at the bank.

Mr Darling had forgotten his umbrella, and since heavy rain was forecast later in the day, Mrs Darling asked Peter if he'd take it to him. After writing the bank's address down for Peter and giving him some change for the tram, she reminded him to be on his best behaviour when he got there.

'Remember, a bank is a very important place. You must be quiet, and don't speak unless you are spoken to.'

'I know,' said Peter. 'Don't worry, I'll be on my best behaviour.' And he was as good as his word, politely asking the receptionist for Mr Darling, before handing over his umbrella.

'Thank you, Peter,' said a grateful Mr Darling, who dreaded the thought of getting drenched on his way home from work. Peter stood with his mouth hanging open as he took in his surroundings. Amazing columns and pillars and fancy lights on the ceiling. It was as if he'd stepped into another world. *I bet inside Buckingham Palace is exactly like this*, he said to himself.

'I see you're impressed, Peter,' said a proud Mr Darling.

'It's spectacular, sir,' replied Peter.

'Well, if you study hard enough, who knows – maybe one day you'll be fortunate enough to work here.'

Peter smiled politely and made his excuses, leaving Mr Darling to his very important job. He strolled home, not taking the direct route, just wandering. Growing up with all these new rules to learn was hard, but at least he enjoyed sightseeing and walks in parks and ice cream. But work? That had never crossed his mind. He wanted to keep learning, especially reading – but work? He liked Mr Darling and had marvelled at the inside of the bank. But work? There?

The thought of being forced to wear a suit and tie all week, being stuck inside a building all day for his entire adult life, filled him with dread, and suddenly he had a very faint memory of being a baby in a pram, and his mother talking, mapping out his future life.

It began to rain. Peter pulled up his jacket collar tight round his neck and kept walking, his shoulders hunched and his head down.

*　*　*

One Sunday afternoon, after a stroll along the Thames and over Tower Bridge, Peter and Wendy took a seat on a bench in St James's Park. She'd brought sandwiches, two slices of cake and a flask of tea.

Children of all ages were playing, and Peter was drawn to the younger boys, flying kites and climbing trees. He longed to join them. He'd been trying so hard to change and grow up, but he couldn't deny the pull – the urge to run and climb.

He smiled as he watched one boy climb. Up he went, lost in his own world, clambering from branch to branch, playing his own game. *Maybe he's searching for pirates*, Peter thought. Suddenly a stern voice shattered the calm scene.

'Come down from there this instant, young man!' called the boy's mother. 'I will not tolerate this sort of behaviour. Look at your trousers, they're all dirty, and your jacket is torn. What will your father say? What will other people think?'

Why would anyone care what other people think? It made little sense to Peter. He watched as the annoyed mother took the boy by the hand and marched him off.

'Just let them be children,' Peter said under his breath. Wendy noticed his reaction, and felt a pang of doubt.

Was she doing the right thing in helping to change him? And if she was, why did she feel guilty?

Late one afternoon, Peter took his lemonade out into the Darlings' back garden. He'd finished his chores for the day, and Wendy was still at school.

Peter loved the back garden, and had been learning the names of the birds. He could now spot not only sparrows, but blue tits, wrens, chaffinches, and his favourite, the blackbirds. Neverland might have been teeming with all manner of birds, from sea eagles to wild parrots, but Peter thought none of them were as handsome as British blackbirds, with their bright yellow beaks and jet-black feathers.

He'd made friends with them, especially one male, who loved raisins. Peter started with throwing raisins on the grass and the bird, whom Peter called 'Blackie', would swoop down for his prize. Gradually, he threw the raisins closer and closer to himself, and finally Blackie landed on Peter's shoulder. Moving ever so carefully so as to not scare it off, Peter fed it a raisin from his hand. It even allowed Peter to stroke its puffed-out chest.

Blackie chirped a thank you and flew off up into the row of conifer trees at the far end of the garden. The flight was perfect, the way the bird soared through the air with such ease . . .

'Wait, a minute . . . I can fly!' he announced to the garden. He glanced around. There was no one there; Mrs Darling must be out on an errand.

Peter ran over to the old cherry tree and climbed up to the second branch, just over five feet off the ground. It felt good to be up a tree again. He closed his eyes and after a pause of three seconds, flung himself off . . . he was in mid-air . . . he was flying . . . and . . . uh-oh, no he wasn't. He hit the ground with a thud.

Dazed and shocked, he picked himself up, brushed the dirt off his trousers and climbed back up the tree, a little higher this time. Around seven feet off the ground.

He closed his eyes, *Come on, you can do it,* and again flung himself off. Again he hit the ground with a thud. His trousers were now covered in grass, his shirt was dirty, and his arms and side hurt. He tried one last time, from ten feet up . . . and *splat!* Down he came, like a sack of bricks. It really hurt this time.

'Peter, what are you doing, you'll break your neck!' a horrified Wendy called from the open patio doors.

Later, as Peter sat in the bathtub in the children's bathroom, he mulled over what had happened in the garden. *Why can't I fly? I used to be able to fly . . .*

Peter Pan really was growing up.

CHAPTER 19

'I want to introduce you to someone, Peter. Our neighbour. He's an author. You'll like him,' said Wendy with a warm smile.

'What's his name?'

'Mr Barrie, Mr J. M. Barrie.'

As Wendy had said, Mr Barrie, a young man in his thirties, was an author. He had a vivid imagination and was a dreamer – some people even thought him a genius.

Wendy herself wanted to become a writer one day, and she spent as much time in Mr Barrie's company as she could.

Until recently, it had always been Wendy bending Mr Barrie's ear, asking him how to find inspiration and what to write about. But that all changed when Wendy started telling him about her trips to Neverland.

Of course, she didn't tell him it was real – he'd never have believed her. Instead, Wendy said they were dreams. Barrie sat in awe as Wendy talked excitedly about a flying boy who turned up at her window one night, and whisked her and her brothers off to an enchanted land called Neverland. He listened in amazement at tales of pirates and their fierce leader, mermaids and all manner of other things.

'This may well be the story that puts me on the map,' Barrie said to himself one night while scribbling in his notebook. 'This is wonderful. How can someone so young possibly dream such wonderful things?' But then again, being young at heart himself, Barrie knew the power of a child's imagination.

He knew he was onto a winner, and with Wendy's permission, he started to compile a book of stories, called 'Wendy in Neverland'. He even planned to turn the stories into a play for the London stage.

'What's so special about this Mr Barrie?' asked Peter.

Wendy explained that Mr Barrie was writing stories based on her 'dreams'.

Peter was excited. 'So he'll write about Neverland? Really?'

'Yes, isn't it wonderful?'

'And will he write about me?'

'Well yes, of course, but . . .'

'But what?'

'We can't tell him who you are – not who you *really* are, I mean.'

'Why not?'

'Peter,' Wendy spoke like a parent to a child, 'can you imagine the conversation? Ah, good morning, Mr Barrie, I'd like to introduce you to Peter Pan. He used to live in Neverland, and one night he flew into my nursery. Then he whisked me off and we flew through the sky. In Neverland we met pirates and the Lost Boys who live in the forest. Oh, and there are witches, not to mention real live talking mermaids . . . and of course it's all true, it really happened.'

'But it *is* true. It *did* happen,' Peter protested.

'Oh Peter, you are so naïve sometimes. Of course *we* know it's true – but you're in London now. People will think we're soft in the head.'

'So, what will we tell this Mr Barrie of yours?'

'Don't worry, I've already discussed it with Mother and Father. We'll say you're a long-lost cousin who has come to stay with us. And don't worry, Mr Barrie is far too much a gentleman to pry.'

Half an hour later, Wendy and Peter walked down the garden path towards Mr Barrie's door. 'Remember Peter, be on your best behaviour. Don't slurp your tea, and never take more than two small cakes. Don't sit before you're offered a seat, and *please* don't burp.'

'Yes, Wendy . . .' *This growing-up lark certainly comes with lots of rules,* Peter thought.

'But most important of all, remember what we agreed about who you are.'

'Peter, the long-lost cousin from Oxford.'

'That's right.' Wendy rapped the door knocker three times, and they waited.

* * *

Mr Barrie's conservatory was a glass room attached to the back of the house that overlooked a large, overgrown garden. The conservatory itself was stuffed full of tropical plants. It was the closest thing to a jungle Peter had experienced since he left Neverland, and he loved it. The London parks were nice enough, but they were too neat and tidy. Mr Barrie's plants, many of which went right up to the glass roof, grew wild, and Peter's mind was soon lost in a sea of green.

The blissful, dreamy look on his face did not go

unnoticed by Wendy, or Mr Barrie. He was glad someone so young enjoyed his plants, but this Peter chap looked as if he were in a trance.

Wendy, sitting to Peter's left, gave him a quick kick under the table, and Peter instantly came out of it.

'I like your plants, sir, very natural.'

'Thank you, Peter.' *Intriguing boy*, Barrie thought.

Peter was on his best behaviour and managed to keep to the script about being the long-lost cousin from Oxford. He managed not to burp while eating his slice of cake, or drop crumbs on his lap. But he did slurp his tea.

'Manners, Cousin Peter, please,' reminded Wendy.

So much to remember, so many rules. 'Sorry, Wendy. Sorry, Mr Barrie.'

Barrie smiled, picked up his own teacup and took an exaggerated slurp. He wanted this shy and unsettled boy to be at ease, so he leaned in towards Peter and with a twinkle in his eye said, 'Tea always tastes better when you slurp.'

He winked, and Peter beamed a huge smile.

For just under an hour, Barrie bombarded Wendy with yet more questions on her Neverland 'dreams'.

'How many times did you have the same dream?' 'Did Neverland and its characters stay the same each time?' 'Explain the mermaids in more detail to me . . . do you think Hook would've made you walk the plank?' 'What's Peter Pan really like? And what does he want from life?'

Wendy did her best to answer, while Peter, on his best behaviour, sat quietly. His mind drifted off though, and he was lost in Barrie's plants, which in his mind's eye turned into a wild jungle. He walked through his imaginary jungle without a care in the world . . .

'I never asked you, Wendy, but did the boy call himself Peter or did you make it up?'

'It was the name he gave himself. He told me on the first night in the nursery.'

'Quite a coincidence then that your young cousin here also goes by the name of Peter,' Barrie said, with a touch of curiosity in his voice.

'Yes, yes, I suppose it is. I hadn't thought about it, to be honest.'

Wendy was genuinely uncomfortable with this. She admired Mr Barrie, and hated lying to him.

'But you must, my dear,' her father had earlier told her. 'People will think you've lost your mind if you claim Neverland is real. Oh no, we can't have that. I mean, what would the bank think?'

Wendy couldn't care less what the bank thought. Perhaps she could confide in Mr Barrie. He'd believe her. Wouldn't he?

Wendy suddenly realised she'd been lost in her own thoughts.

'And what about you, young Peter?' asked Barrie.

'Sir?' Peter had not been listening either, still lost in the jungle in his mind's eye.

'What do you think, about your cousin's dreams and her tales of flying off to Neverland?'

Wendy looked at Peter, hoping he'd manage stay in character.

'They are . . . interesting, sir.'

A strange answer for a boy to give. The kind of thing an adult might say. Was he holding something back?

Barrie continued. 'Neverland sounds such a marvellous place. To live on a paradise island where boys never have to obey rules and never have to grow up. I bet you'd like to go there, wouldn't you Peter? And to have your own real live talking fairy?'

Peter shrugged. 'Not really, sir. A place like that, it's not for me.' He smiled, a half-nervous smile. An awkward moment passed before Barrie stood up and broke the silence.

'Well, that's enough brain-picking for one day. Another pot of tea, anyone?'

'Yes please,' said Wendy, and Peter added, sounding like a much younger boy, 'And more cakes please!'

Mr Barrie smiled and headed off to the kitchen.

What was it about this boy that was so intriguing? A long-lost distant cousin? Barrie wasn't so sure. Wendy had no reason to lie, but something didn't sit right. Peter was a truly fascinating boy. He had a faraway look in his eye, and seemed to be hiding something, or holding something back. Barrie was convinced that, somehow or other, he was not being told the truth about Cousin Peter.

* * *

As the months passed, the boy once known as Peter Pan became unrecognisable.

His manners were excellent, he walked with his back straight, and never slurped his tea. He never climbed trees again, nor did he try to fly.

He was almost a young man.

Having put so much effort into this transformation of Peter, you'd think Wendy would be delighted with the result. But no. She had exactly what she'd wished for, but now she wasn't sure who she loved more, the Peter who stood before her – the one she'd helped to create – or the Peter of old, the one she'd tried to change.

Peter no longer had flashbacks or nightmares, and he no longer sat in parks with his mind drifting off. He remembered Neverland, but it was as if his mind had put his past in a box at the far corner of his memory, locked it and thrown away the key. When Wendy did occasionally bring it up in general chat, he simply went quiet until the conversation finished.

To the casual observer – even to Mr and Mrs Darling – Peter was just a well-mannered, well-behaved, normal boy. A happy boy.

Wendy was sceptical, though. She desperately wanted to believe that everything was OK with him, but deep down she worried it was all an act.

CHAPTER 20

It was now six months since Peter had left Neverland. Although the boys initially hoped he'd come back, that hope had faded with every passing week. Tootles was in charge now, but it didn't feel right. Nothing was right anymore. They went about their business as best they could, but their hearts weren't in it. Their hearts were broken.

To say Hook was depressed would be the understatement of the year. When Tink woke him up that fateful morning and told him the news, it hit him like a brick and sent him spiralling back downwards. Smee helped him back to Pirate Cove, and onto the *Jolly Roger*. The pirates – those who still remained – tried to cheer him up. They even repaired the ship and restored it to its former glory, but to no avail. Hook just sat in his cabin and drank rum.

As for Tinkerbell, she'd had it worst of all. She'd saved Peter's life as a baby and brought him to Neverland, looked after him, taught him how to fly. She'd done everything for him. And this was how he repaid her? By abandoning her?

If only. If only Peter had found them that night. If he'd just seen them with Hook, this disaster would never have happened.

Tink had planned to fly to London and create havoc for Wendy, but both Ilba and Migizi persuaded her not to. At first, Tink was angry with the chief for writing that letter for Peter, but she soon got over it. Migizi was one of the good guys, she knew that.

'If Peter is to come back, he must do so of his own accord, or it won't be genuine,' Migizi told her. She knew it made sense, but she still believed that Wendy had a hold over Pan, and was filling his head with nonsense about love and growing up.

She needed to do something. She could not – would not – let it rest.

'This can't be it,' she said to Ilba one morning, 'Surely it all doesn't end here, not like this . . .'

Ilba thought long and hard before replying. 'You need to use your secret weapon.'

'What are you talking about, Ilba? You sound like Migizi. Stop talking in riddles.'

'Hook.'

'Hook what? What do you mean?'

'He is your secret weapon. Think about it. Before Pan left, what was the one thing you claimed would bring him to his senses and make him want to have adventures again? It was Hook. We brought him back, but of course, it was too late.'

'I know this, Ilba!' Tink was getting frustrated. But Ilba continued calmly.

'Think. Pan doesn't know that Hook has returned to Neverland, does he? If he did, it might still change everything. Hook is still your secret weapon, your trump card. You've got to use him. You've got nothing to lose.'

Ilba was right. But how? What could she do? She could fly to London and try to persuade him . . . but no, that wouldn't work, Pan would never believe her that Hook had somehow come back from the dead and miraculously returned to Neverland.

Tink thanked Ilba and flew off. This needed thought . . .

* * *

Late the next afternoon, Tink flew into Pirate Cove.

'Tinkerbell! What a lovely surprise!' said a genuinely happy Smee. Why he worked for Hook, Tink couldn't understand.

'I need to speak with Hook.'

Smee scratched his chin. 'Hmm,' he said. 'He's not in a good way.'

'Who is these days?'

Smee nodded in agreement. 'He's sleeping, he sleeps all the time now . . . even during the day. He's even more depressed than when we were stuck on that island. What is it you want to speak with him about?'

'I have a plan, but I need his help. Will you help me, Mr Smee? I've always found you such a nice helpful pirate . . .' She said it in such a flirty way that Smee simply couldn't resist.

'I'll go and wake him up. You stay right here!'

Hook was not best pleased to be roused from his afternoon slumber. Once Smee had got him propped up in bed, with his wig on and false teeth in, he ushered in Tinkerbell, who flew in and landed on the bedpost at the bottom of Hook's bed.

Hook looked awful. He was unshaven and had dark circles under his eyes.

Tink told him she had a plan she needed his help with, but he didn't even react. 'C'mon Hook,' she tried a different ploy, 'this is not like you. I mean, lying in your bed in the daytime. Where's the captain we live in fear of? The captain we secretly admire?'

'Admire?' This caught Hook's attention. Tink smiled. She walked up and down the entire breadth of Hook's bed as he sat, watching her closely.

'Sure, I admire you Hook. Even though we're on opposite sides, I've always thought of you as a foe to be admired.'

'How so?'

'Well, you're brave. Very brave. I mean, after that croc took your hand many years ago, then chased and followed you, a lesser man would have crumbled, but not you, not the great Captain Hook . . .'

'Go on,' said Hook, enjoying the praise.

'I've always admired you from afar. I used to say to Pan that we'd never get the better of Hook because he's just too powerful. Too organised and an outstanding leader. We lived in fear. We always feared that one day you'd find our hideout.'

Tink studied Hook's reaction . . . it was exactly as she'd hoped. She continued, 'And I'll let you into a secret . . .'

'What?' asked Hook, sitting up and leaning forward. He was enjoying this.

'Even Peter Pan respected you. It's true! He often said to me he'd never be able to beat old Hook, and before Wendy first arrived, he even considered surrendering to you. Simply because he knew that in the end, you would win and take over Neverland.'

Despite enjoying the flattery and praise, Hook was no fool.

'I'll give you ten out of ten for trying, Miss Bell,' he said sarcastically. Then added with a sigh, 'Go on then, tell me your plan.'

She did. And Hook sat quietly and listened until she finished.

* * *

'So, what do you think? C'mon, come with me, Hook. Work with me. We'll go to London and convince Pan to return to Neverland.'

Hook was interested but hesitant. Tink flew up closer and landed on the tea tray that Smee had placed on his lap. She looked up at him and pleaded, 'Let's work together for once. We both want the same thing after all, don't we?'

'Keep your friends close, but your enemies even closer?'

Tink thought for a moment before replying, 'I've never been sure what that actually means, but yeah, if you wish.' She then smiled a seductive smile and asked, 'Did you grow a new moustache?'

'What do you mean?'

'Your moustache. It's different, fuller – makes you look stronger, even more masculine than usual. I like it.'

Hook toyed with his moustache, and once again couldn't help but succumb to flattery. 'Yes, I grew it . . .'

'And it suits you. Very striking indeed.'

Men, she thought. *So vain.*

Hook was still stroking his new moustache when he asked, 'And how do you propose we get to London? Listen, Miss Bell, many years ago I spent months on a ship getting away from there. I haven't been in London since, and I'm not spending weeks on another boat trying to get back.'

'Don't worry, I'll take care of that. But if you agree, you'll have to go in disguise.'

'How do you mean?'

'Well, look at you. You can't walk around London looking like Long John Silver.'

'But I love my clothes. I'm splendid in them.'

'Of course you are.' Back on the charm offensive, she flew up, landed on his shoulder and gently stroked the lapel of his jacket. 'But for this secret operation, you must be in disguise. Oh, and the hook has to go.'

'But it's my trademark! It's who I am!'

'You'll create terror if you walk around London with a hook for a hand.'

'Create terror, you say . . .' This appealed to Hook. Tink flew back down to the tea tray.

'You must focus on our goal! We're going so we can bring Peter Pan back to Neverland, not on a trip for you to create mischief.'

Like a little boy being scolded by a teacher, Hook, with a sulky face, reluctantly nodded in agreement.

Tink realised she needed to keep him keen, so she promised him something that Hook had wanted to do for years.

'Hook, my new chum,' Tink announced. 'You are going to fly to London.'

His face lit up and his eyes sparkled.

'Well, not exactly fly, something even better. I'm going to make you disappear from Neverland, and then reappear in London.'

'You can do that?'

'Sure I can, it's fairy magic. I'm very clever, you know. But you need to help me.'

Hook sat bolt upright in bed. 'Anything you say, Miss Bell.'

'First, get up and get dressed. Time is short, we must leave tonight. I need to go now, but I'll be back in an hour. I'll meet on the deck of the ship. OK?'

Hook nodded enthusiastically.

She wagged a tiny finger at him. 'Don't be late Hook, we have a big journey ahead of us.'

'I won't be late, I'll be ready. Smee? Mr Smee, get my best jacket and boots ready. I'm going to London!'

So easy, thought Tink as she flew off. *So gullible. Toss him a few compliments, tell him what he wants to hear and hey presto, he's putty in your hand.*

* * *

One hour later, immaculately dressed, Hook was itching to get going.

'Bravo, Hook, you look splendid,' said Tink as she landed on a barrel next to where he was standing.

'I'm ready, Miss Bell. What happens now?'

Tink had a quick glance to her left, then her right. Apart from Hook and Smee, there were four other men on board.

'Send your men away, I don't want any of them to see this.'

'Right, you horrible lot, make yourselves scarce. Here, take this,' Hook delved into his coat pocket, and threw a handful of coins in their direction. 'Take yourselves off to the tavern. Hook's paying!'

It was the first time he'd ever done that, and his astonished men were nearly speechless, apart from thanking him a dozen times.

Once they were gone, Tink looked at Hook. 'Right, we're ready. Stand still.'

She flew up and over Hook's head, sprinkling fairy dust that cascaded down all over him.

Hook sneezed, and wiped his nose on his sleeve.

'Now we fly?'

'No, it's not as simple as that.'

Like an impatient child, Hook snapped, 'So what now?'

'Now I need you to believe. And I need you to think happy thoughts.'

'He doesn't have any,' said Smee matter-of-factly.

Hook frowned, but he wasn't sure what to make of that comment, so he let it pass.

'You must have,' replied Tink. 'Come on, think: what makes you happy?'

Hook thought for a moment. 'Killing Peter Pan!'

Tink was outraged. 'Bad form, Hook! Bad form!'

'Sorry, Miss Bell,' he apologised, but with a wicked glint in his eye.

For ten long minutes Hook tried but failed to come up with happy thoughts. Well, happy thoughts that were acceptable to Tink. Driving the Opacanta from Neverland, Tink could not accept. Pulling the wings off butterflies got him a scolding. Drowning the mermaids in their own lagoon . . . oh no, that would not do either. Boiling the witches in their own cauldrons . . . now Tink nearly accepted that one.

Finally, just as her patience was running out, Hook turned to her and said. 'I've got it, Miss Bell! My happy thought is . . . Peter Pan back in Neverland, and me chasing him through the forests, a fight to the end for the undisputed right to rule Neverland.'

That was good enough, and Tink nodded her approval. Suddenly Hook slowly rose, till he was suspended about two feet off the ground. 'Miss Bell, you are a genius, I am floating off the ground!'

Tink pointed her tiny finger, teacher-style. 'Listen to me Hook, no nonsense. I'm in charge of this operation, agreed?'

Hook, floating in the air and beside himself with excitement, nodded in agreement.

'No harming Peter Pan, no fighting or mischief in London. Agreed?'

Hook nodded energetically, desperate to get going.

'And to make sure you do behave, I'll be coming with you.'

'Do you know where Pan is?'

'At Wendy's house, of course.'

Tink joined him at eye level and waved her tiny wand over both their heads. Within seconds, they'd started to disintegrate into tiny specks of light.

Smee was dumbstruck at the sight.

'Good luck Tinkerbell! Good luck Cap'n!' he cried out. 'Bring Pan back, Godspeed!'

Seconds later, both Hook and Tink disappeared.

* * *

Tink had explained her plan to the Lost Boys earlier.

'Why not, what do we have to lose?' said Tootles. 'Go for it, Tink!' Then, quietly and with heartfelt emotion, 'I do like being leader, but . . . I'd rather have Peter here. Bring him back, Tink, please bring him back.' The rest of the boys nodded in agreement.

'I'll do my best, boys.'

After finishing their supper, the Lost Boys got into their beds and settled down for the night. It had been an awful six months, but they were confident that Tink would return with Peter Pan. And then, surely, life would finally get back to normal.

'Goodnight Neverland!' Tootles shouted as he released the fireflies from his glass jar.

Enveloped within the safety of darkness, where no witches could find them, the only sounds in Neverland's inner jungle were from the creatures and insects of the night. And the odd snoring Lost Boy of course.

CHAPTER 21

It took a moment or two until Hook felt his physical body and got his bearings. He checked himself over, touching his face and arms and legs. Yes, everything was there and in one piece. How Tinkerbell had managed it, he did not know. But she had, and he now stood in a dark alleyway down by the docks, close to London's River Thames. An area he remembered well, from a long time ago.

'You all right, Hook?' asked Tinkerbell

'Where are you? I can't see you.'

'I'm here,' said a voice,

'Where?'

Suddenly Hook felt a tap on his right shoulder. He turned to face Tink, not as a fairy, but as a small bright light.

'Why don't you show yourself?'

'I don't think London society is ready to see a real live fairy, do you?'

'I guess not.'

'And remember, it's definitely not ready to see a pirate captain either. That's why I've changed your clothes.'

Hook hadn't noticed. He looked himself over once again. Gone were the clothes that Smee had sorted out for him.

139

Instead, he now wore a suit, a shirt and tie, and black shoes. With a long black overcoat, he looked every inch the English gentleman.

'But you forgot one thing . . .'

Tink was perplexed. 'What?'

'This,' he said, holding up his gleaming hook.

'Oh, yeah. Well, that definitely has to go.'

For the next five minutes they had a heated discussion about what to do with the hook. Imagine the scene: a grown man, standing in an alleyway, having a conversation with a glowing light on his shoulder.

The homeless man in a corner not so far away lay with one eye open, watching the spectacle. But he could neither see nor hear Tink, so to him it looked like the man was speaking to himself.

'Take off your hook.'

He protested.

'Take it off.'

'I shan't!' He sounded like Peter when Nana was trying to get him into the bath on a Sunday evening.

'Hook, you agreed! Now, listen to me, if you don't do this, it's back to Neverland with you in an instant. And then we'll never find Pan and that will be the end of that.'

Not happy, but knowing he had no choice, Hook mumbled his reluctant acceptance. The homeless man was lying still, wondering who this strange gentleman having a conversation with himself was.

But when the strange figure undid some straps on his arm and unclasped a huge, shiny metal hook, the homeless man took a sharp intake of breath, before clamping his hand over his mouth. This was no gentleman . . . this was a monster!

He'd seen enough. As quietly as possible, praying he'd not be noticed, he pulled his blanket over his head and closed his eyes as tight as he could.

'What now? I can't walk around with only one working hand, and the other wrist dangling limp by my side. It is not becoming.'

'Agreed,' said Tink. She thought for a minute. 'Right, close your eyes. This might sting a bit.'

'What are going to do to me?'

'Oh, stop being a big baby. Close your eyes.' He did, but two seconds later opened one eye to get a peek.

'Both eyes, Hook,' Tink scolded him. He finally did as he was told.

After a sprinkling of fairy dust and a wave of her wand, a rubber hand magically appeared, attached to the end of the captain's arm.

Hook was not impressed. It looked fake, useless, dead.

'It's the best I can do under the circumstances,' said Tink, reminding him that he couldn't be Captain Hook here, any more than she could be a real live fairy.

'Our job is to find Pan, remember? Then, and only then, can we both change back into our ourselves. Got it?'

Although he wasn't happy, he reluctantly agreed. 'Very well,' he grunted.

'It will take time though to get used to this damn thing,' he said as he held up his fake hand. 'It looks pathetic, and it doesn't even move.'

Fed up with his moaning, Tink remarked, 'Then buy a pair of gloves.'

'And what about my hook? You can't expect me to walk around all day carrying it.'

'Oh for goodness' sake.' This was like dealing with a

child. 'Find a bag or something to stick it in. I don't know.'

Yes, first thing tomorrow, that's what he'd do. He find a bag, a good bag, to carry his precious hook in. He refused to let it leave his sight, and Tinkerbell was not getting her hands on it. No way.

That was a problem for tomorrow, but what about tonight? Hook took a good hard look at his surroundings. Cold, dank, smelly and nearly pitch-black.

'Where, may I ask, are we going to sleep tonight?'

'I can sleep anywhere, I'm tiny, remember.'

'But what about me?' he protested. 'It's cold. I can't sleep outside, I'll freeze to death.'

He had a point.

'Wait here, I'll see what I can find.' Off she flew, leaving Hook standing alone in the dark alleyway.

As Hook attempted to pull his jacket tightly round himself, his fake hand fell off and landed in a dirty puddle.

He cursed, picked it up, wiped it dry and stuck it back on his stump. It rubbed painfully, and jabbed at the nerve endings. He'd have to make it fit better, but all he wanted right then was to be warm and get some sleep. *Where was that damn fairy?*

Suddenly a voice in his ear announced, 'Come on, I've found a place.' Tink took off and Hook followed her tiny glowing light. Down the alley and into another, which was even smaller than the last. Finally, at the end, stood an old storage building with a broken lock. She flew in.

Hook tentatively opened the door and peered inside.

'Come on, it's safe, don't be scared now,' she said with a giggle.

'I am *not* scared. What a ridiculous suggestion.'

'Whatever. Come on, over here.' She led him to a corner where old sacks were piled up against a wall. Hook breathed in the scent. They were sacks of tobacco. What a wonderful smell – he suddenly craved a good cigar. It had been such a long time.

'Well . . . not exactly the Savoy, but it will do, I suppose. But for one night only. You can't expect the great Captain James Hook to sleep in here.'

'Oh give it a rest, Hook. This is all I can find at short notice. At least it's dry in here.'

She was right, it was dry, and by making himself a bed on the sacks of tobacco leaves, it might just be tolerable. As he pulled and dragged at the sacks with his good hand, he thought to himself that this was not how he had envisaged spending his first night back in London.

With his bed finally made, and using another thick sack of tobacco leaves as a pillow, Hook lay down.

'Miss Bell? Where the devil are you now?'

No reply. Apart from the sound of snoring. Perched on a nearby wooden shelf, covered in bits of tobacco and straw, Tinkerbell was already fast asleep.

'For someone so small, you can certainly snore, Miss Bell.'

Because she couldn't sustain her light glow for long periods of time, Tink was now back in her physical form.

Hook reached out his good hand to within inches from her, 'I could squash her like a bug, right here and now,' he thought to himself, but then pulled back. 'No, that would most definitely be bad form.' Besides, he needed her. For the time being.

'But once I've found Pan and dragged him back to Neverland, things will change . . .'

He pulled one more empty cloth sack over his body and closed his eyes. But sleep didn't come, only thoughts of the past. Hook's mind was a swirl of thoughts and emotions from his life in London long ago. He remembered running away from the orphanage, and sleeping in a slum area of London, possibly not far away from where he was now. Remembered a hard upbringing, having to steal to survive. Most of all, he remembered his mother, who had abandoned him, who had chosen his older brother over him. A mother who didn't love him. Suddenly Hook felt very lonely indeed.

He pushed those sad thoughts away, they did him no good. He needed to focus on the here and now.

There is no way I am spending another night in here, his internal voice said with authority. Not knowing how long it would take to find Pan, he decided he'd need to find a room with a proper bed for a start. But to do that he needed money, and he had none. He needed to get cash and fast.

A thin, wicked grin soon spread across his lips.

'Yes, I'm sure I can remember how to pick a pocket or two,' he said to himself with pride.

Hook yawned, and moments later joined Tinkerbell in that mysterious land of deep sleep.

* * *

'Where have you been?' asked Tink the next morning, as she sat up and rubbed her eyes.

'I've been up for hours, Miss Bell. Out in the big bad world, getting organised.'

Tink yawned and enjoyed a scratch. 'What have you got there?' she asked, pointing at the small pile Hook had just placed on the floor.

'Goodies, Miss Bell. Lots of goodies.'

'Where did you get them from?'

'Where do you think?'

'You stole them?' Tink was about to give him a stern telling-off, but Hook raised his fake hand and cut her off before she could speak.

'Don't give me any of your sanctimonious claptrap, Miss Bell. And remember, people in glass houses shouldn't throw stones.'

'What do you mean?' Tink was on the defensive.

'Don't tell me you'd never steal?'

'I certainly would not!'

'Really? Then please explain who stole all manner of items from the *Jolly Roger* over the years? Hmm? Cups, plates, candles, matches, food, a hairbrush, clocks and even one poor pirate's wooden leg.'

Hook gave her a knowing look. Tink went bright red and gave an embarrassed smile, while Hook enjoyed his victory. He then took much pleasure in showing her his ill-gotten gains.

'First, a fine leather bag, which I will use to carry my hook in. Splendid, isn't it?'

'What's inside the bag?'

'A very expensive pocket watch. Not sure if I'll keep it or pawn it. A thick wallet stuffed full of cash, which I will definitely be keeping, and using to buy myself some luxury. And I've also acquired a very fetching cane.'

'Busy morning, I see.'

'A very satisfactory start to the day, I'd say.'

Tink tutted at this display of thievery, but then suddenly stopped and sniffed. 'What's that smell?'

'Breakfast,' said Hook. 'Fresh bread, hot out of the baker's oven.'

'And you stole that as well?'

'Of course,' said Hook proudly. 'And a pint of milk swiped from a doorstep just moments ago.' He ripped off a chunk of the bread, and stuffed it into his mouth.

Tink sat and stared at him, like a hungry pet dog. Hook sensed he was being watched, and glanced sideways at her. He stopped chewing and screwed up his face at her puppy-dog eyes.

'I didn't get you anything, sorry. I mean . . . well, I don't know what fairies eat.' He shoved another piece of warm bread into his mouth, before adding, 'What do fairies eat?'

'Same as you, only smaller amounts.'

Hook grumbled to himself, shook his head, tore off a small piece of bread and handed it to her. It was small to him, but nearly the size of Tink herself. She thanked him and greedily gobbled it down.

Hook watched her with fascination. *Such a tiny little thing . . . where does she put it all?* he wondered.

'Milk, please!' announced Tinkerbell.

Hook glanced around the floor looking for something to put it in and found an old bottle top. He poured in a splash of milk and handed it to her. Tink carefully lifted the bottle top to her mouth with both hands and gulped the lot, before flinging the bottle top Frisbee-style right across the room. She wiped the milk moustache from her face, smacked her lips and finally gave a huge burp of satisfaction.

'Bad form, Miss Bell!' He attempted to scold her, but a tiny smile escaped from the side of his mouth.

'So what now?' asked Hook. 'We are here for a purpose.'

Tink, fully rested after a good night's sleep and refreshed after her breakfast, stood up and stretched.

'We go and find Peter Pan.'

'That's the spirit! Now, lead on.'

'What do you mean, lead on?'

'To find Pan, lead on and take me to him.'

'But I don't know where he is.'

'What?'

'Well I do, he's at Wendy's of course.'

'Then take me there.'

'Bit of a problem . . . kind of difficult . . .'

'What do you mean?'

'I'm not *exactly* sure where she lives. You see, I've always followed Pan when he came here . . .'

As you can imagine, there then followed a good five minutes of ranting and raving by both parties, before Hook called for calm.

'But you've been there before. You must remember something. Tell me what you remember about the house?'

'Well . . . it's got a chimney, lots of chimneys. Does that help?'

Hook, knowing that every house in London's West End boasted a set of chimneys, said sternly, 'No, Miss Bell, it does not help.'

'So what are we to do then?' Tink rested her chin in her hands glumly.

'We get out onto the streets, that's the only thing for it. Never forget who I am. I am a pirate . . . and if I can find buried treasure on a desert island, I can find Peter Pan in London.'

He stood up and slung the bag over his shoulder. With back straight and head held high, he announced, 'Let us go, London awaits.'

And with that, and the cane swinging in his good hand, he strutted out through the gap in the door and into the alleyway.

Tink shrugged a *Why not?* and flew off to join him.

Heading in the general direction of central London, Hook walked briskly and with purpose. He was determined to succeed in his mission. But London was such a big city. Where on earth to even start?

'To catch your prey, you must think like your prey,' Hook said to himself. Now where, he wondered, would a young boy go in London . . .

CHAPTER 22

'My feet are sore,' complained Hook as he sat down on a bench on the Embankment by the Thames.

'My wings hurt,' added Tink, who rested herself on Hook's left shoulder.

They'd been at it for three weeks, three long weeks. Up and down nearly every street in London's West End, yet still no sign of Peter Pan.

'Is this the street?' asked Hook for the umpteenth time that day.

'They all look the same to me,' came the reply, for the umpteenth time that day.

Hook tried to fathom out where a young boy like Pan would go in London. Surely he wouldn't spend his days inside a house? But having never had a childhood of his own, he had no idea.

'A museum?'

'No way,' said Tink.

'Down by the Thames to see the ships?'

'Possibly . . .'

They walked all over the docks, but never saw him. Plenty of other kids around, but no one resembling Pan – although that hadn't stopped Hook from grabbing the odd boy by the arm and whisking him round to get a better look at his face. Tink scolded him for that.

'I know,' said Tink, 'the zoo.'

They duly visited London Zoo, but of course there was no sign of Peter. Frustrating as this was, Hook enjoyed his visit to the zoo. They say that animals can pick up on human feelings – and even sense evil. When Hook walked past the monkey enclosure, a mix of fear and fury enveloped them, especially the baboons. They screamed and hissed at him. It was a terrifying display, which scared the nearby children. The zookeeper later claimed he'd never seen such a reaction. Hook revelled in it.

'This is pointless,' Hook admitted as he rubbed his feet. 'I mean, we not only have to find a place where Pan might go, we also have to be in that place at the exact time he's there.'

They both agreed they needed a Plan B.

* * *

Hook rented a room in the Holborn area of central London. The owner agreed a price and Hook paid a week in advance. It wasn't luxury, but it was clean, with a bed and running water.

They spent the daytime out looking for Pan, and in the evenings, Hook sampled the rum in the surrounding pubs. Tink went with him once, but didn't go back, she didn't enjoy it; it smelled like the tavern in Pirate Cove.

Although their frustration at not being able to find Peter Pan grew with each day, they not only tolerated each other, but got on surprisingly well. Once sworn enemies, they bonded in their common cause. What the Lost Boys would have made of it all, Tink couldn't imagine.

'Here, take this.' Hook passed a tiny sliver of chocolate to Tink, after breaking off a sizeable chunk for himself and putting it in his mouth.

'I hope you bought this chocolate bar?' said Tink. 'I mean, you've stolen enough wallets to be able to pay for it.'

Hook ignored the sarcastic comment and told the story of the chocolate bar. 'A child came out of a sweet shop, a well-to-do child, so full of innocence. She put the chocolate in her coat pocket and waited to cross the road. I chanced to be passing by and, well, in one swift move, it was mine. The child never even noticed.' He chomped off another big bite and savoured his treat.

'You're such a wicked man, Hook.'

'Why, thank you, Miss Bell.'

'I didn't mean it as a compliment.'

Hook smiled.

* * *

Hook walked along yet another affluent West End street. They did indeed all look the same. Suddenly, Tink tugged on Hook's shoulder.

'Hang on . . .'

'What?'

'Something . . . I'm not sure . . .'

'You recognise this street?'

Tink looked hard. She didn't physically recognise the street, but she felt something – a pull towards it. She focused on number 42 and looked up at the top floor.

'Wait here.' Tink flew up to the top window, and peered in. It looked more like a young adult's room than a nursery. Yet she was sure it was the same place . . . the same place where she'd witnessed Peter and Wendy kissing. Oh, that still made her blood boil. She shook off these annoying thoughts and flew back down to Hook.

'I think I've found it . . . what do we do now?'

'We wait,' said Hook.

'For what?

'For Pan, that's what.'

They waited over an hour, but no one entered or left the house.

Hook was wary of attracting unwanted attention. The last thing he needed was for a neighbour to contact the police, worried about a man loitering around outside their house. Just when he considered leaving, the front door of the Darlings' neighbour's house opened.

A smartly dressed gentleman held the door open for an elderly woman. His mother maybe? No, she looked more like a servant. The man guided the woman along the path and opened the garden gate for her. Hook, who was trying to look as if he were just another gentleman out for a stroll, bent down to tie his shoelace. Difficult with a fake hand. As he did, he overheard their conversation.

'You're as kind as ever, sir,' said the old woman as she took the money the gentleman held out.

'Not at all, Mary, you are a blessing. My house simply wouldn't function without you. And,' he said, producing a bottle from behind his back, 'here, take this port as a treat.'

'You're too good to me, sir.'

'Same time on Monday?'

'Same time sir, I'll be here.'

'Have yourself an enjoyable weekend, Mary.'

'And you, sir. Thank you, Mr Barrie, thank you, sir.'

The old woman hurried off down the street. The gentleman watched her go, smiled, closed the garden gate and walked back along the path towards his front door.

'Excuse me, sir? May I have a word?'

Barrie stopped and turned round to face the man standing on the pavement outside his garden gate.

'What can I do for you?'

With his best friendly smile, Hook said, 'I'm from out of town and am embarrassed to say that I find myself somewhat lost.'

'Where are you trying to find?'

'Actually I'm looking for an old friend. I wrote the address on a piece of paper, but I must have mislaid it.'

'What's the name of the family you're looking for?'

'The Darling family. We are old family friends . . .'

Worth a try. Anyway, if Tink had been mistaken and picked the wrong street, no harm done, they'd just have to keep looking elsewhere.

'Well, you're in luck, sir. This is their house,' Barrie said as he pointed next door.

A wicked thin grin appeared across Hook's face, but he instantly shook it off and re-composed himself. It had not gone unnoticed by Barrie, though, who seemed a trifle suspicious.

'And you are, sir?' asked Barrie, now sounding like a responsible, concerned neighbour.

Hook smiled, tipped his hat and gave his original name. 'Mr Crook.'

'A pleasure to meet you, Mr Crook. My name is Mr Barrie. But I'm afraid there's no one home next door at present. Can I take a message and pass it on when they return?'

'Oh no, that won't be necessary. Do you know when the family will return?' Hook tentatively asked, trying hard not to push his luck.

'Well, Mrs Darling is out on errands, so I really don't know, it may be any moment. Mr Darling usually returns from the bank at around six in the evening.'

'And what about their daughter, Wendy? Is she home?' Trying so hard to be nice exhausted him.

Tink, a tiny little light out of sight in the brim of his hat, was egging him on with encouraging words. It took all of Hook's concentration not to whip his hat off and tell her to shut up.

But Mr Barrie didn't feel at all comfortable dishing out private information to a stranger on the street.

'You say you know Wendy?' Now he sounded like a protective uncle.

'Why yes, of course. As I mentioned, I'm a friend of the family.'

'Forgive me for asking, but can you describe Wendy to me?'

'I totally understand, sir,' said Hook, hiding his annoyance, and described Wendy in the best detail he could remember. It seemed to be enough to set Barrie's mind at ease.

'I believe she's also out at the moment. Gone for a walk in one of London's parks, as she often does. Her favourite these days is Kensington Gardens. Oh, and she'll most likely be with her cousin Peter.'

Tink sat bolt upright and started excitedly whispering in Hook's ear. 'It's him! It's him!'

As if trying to swat a fly, Hook brushed at the air around his ear and smiled at Barrie.

'Peter, you say?'

'Yes. Are you acquainted with Peter?'

'A cousin, you say?' Hook was playing for time and finally added, 'I am of course aware of the young chap, but have not had the pleasure of his company. Yet . . .'

'My apologies, but I must be going, Mr Crook. I have work to do. But I'll let the family know you came by . . .'

'Oh no!' said Hook, a trifle too abruptly. In a gentler voice he quickly added, 'I'd prefer if you didn't. I haven't seen them for some time, so I'd like it to be a surprise. They will be so happy to see me. I do hope you understand?'

'As you wish,' confirmed Barrie.

Hook raised his hat and called out, 'Good form, sir!'

A strange thing to say, but Barrie nodded his head in acknowledgement.

'I've taken up enough of your time. I thank you, sir, and I hope we will meet again.'

Hook took off, walking briskly down the street and away from the house. Barrie walked to the end of his path and leaned over his front gate, watching the man, who now seemed to be having a conversation with his shoulder. Barrie scratched his chin and shrugged. Probably just eccentric.

Once she'd calmed down, Tink said, 'Right, let's go and find Pan.'

'No. Not now, not yet.'

'But why?'

'We can't just rush in, we must pick the right moment. Meanwhile, we bide our time. There's no hurry. We know where Pan lives, and we also know, according to that annoying neighbour, that Pan likes to walk in Kensington Gardens.'

'Then let's go right now!'

'No,' replied Hook, with calm authority. 'Revenge is a dish best served cold, Miss Bell.'

This made Tink uneasy.

Hook flashed a thin, unnerving smile before adding, 'Don't worry, my dear, it's only a matter of time before we both get *exactly* what we want.'

Tink heard Tootles' voice in her head, 'Remember who he is Tink, he is Hook. I wouldn't trust him as far as I could throw him . . .'

* * *

Back inside the house, Barrie sat at his desk. His writing pad was opened at the beginning of chapter five of 'Wendy in Neverland'. To refresh his memory, he read through what he'd written earlier that morning. Peter Pan and Hook having yet another sword fight on the deck of the *Jolly Roger*. Pan managed to send Hook's sword flying out of his hand. The pirates gasped, the Lost Boys gasped. Was this the end of Hook? No, for in true Neverland style, Pan picked up and threw the sword towards Hook. He'd given him a lifeline.

Captain Hook beamed an enormous smile and called out, 'Good form, Peter, good form!'

Wait a minute. Barrie took off his glasses and laid them gently on the writing table.

Good form? That was the phrase the eccentric gentleman had just used. Certainly not a common phrase in London. In fact, Barrie knew of no one who used it. And now he'd heard it in the flesh from that man on the street. *Interesting coincidence . . .*

Barrie cast his mind back to the strange gentleman.

Why had he called his neighbour 'Mr Darling' and not used his Christian name, George? Strange, when he was claiming to be a friend . . .

There was something mysterious about this man. Barrie had to admit that he felt the same when it came to Cousin Peter. What *was* he not being told?

He shook off those thoughts and began writing again.

* * *

The Lamb and Flag is one of London's oldest pubs. Tucked away at the end of a tiny narrow street, just round the corner from Covent Garden, it is said to date back to the seventeenth century.

In need of refreshment, Hook entered and chose a small table tucked away under an alcove in the far corner. He ate a plate of hot beef stew, washing it down with two glasses of Navy Rum. Not as good as the rum the pirates made themselves back in Neverland, but not bad.

An hour later, Hook left and turned into the tiny passageway that ran parallel to the pub. Being extremely narrow, if someone was walking the other way, you had to stand side-on to let them pass.

As Hook stood at the far end just round the corner from the pub, he lit a cigar and exhaled a billow of thick smoke to the arched bricks overhead, causing the smoke to fall back down, covering him in a grey, hazy shroud.

Mary Morgan, aged sixty-five, a cleaner, was on her way home from her third cleaning job of the day. Her first job started at six in the morning when she cleaned a school. By midday she had moved onto a private household, the home of the author Mr Barrie. A kind man, he not only paid the going rate, but often gave her a small gift of fresh fruit or occasionally a bottle of port. Luxuries indeed for someone like Mary.

At four in the afternoon she attended her last job of the day, to scrub and clean the inside of a butcher's shop in Covent Garden. Undoubtedly hard work, especially the blood-stained chopping boards and huge meat cleavers. But it was worth it, even if Mary didn't get paid any actual money – for this job, she got the pick of whatever was left lying around unsold.

Every day was different. It could be sausages, sometimes beef bones for broth, and if she was very lucky, a piece of actual red meat. Today, Mary had received as payment two large, juicy pork chops, as well as some scraps of chicken for her cat. It was a good deal for both the butcher and Mary.

Mary usually walked home, but today with a bitter winter chill seeping into her old bones, she had decided to treat herself and take a tram instead.

To catch the number nine tram round by Piccadilly, she took a shortcut and walked along the tiny passageway beside the Lamb and Flag.

Hook recognised her instantly. The woman who had been leaving the house next door to the Darlings'.

As Mary approached, she glanced up at the dark figure blocking the alleyway. Dressed in a long black coat with smoke billowing around him, she couldn't make out his face.

With insoles in his shoes to make himself look taller, he stood at six feet, towering over Mary.

'Time to have some fun,' whispered Hook, as he flicked his cigar butt onto the path in front of her. Mary stopped as Hook extinguished the cigar under the heel of his boot.

A lamp lighter had just lit a lamp twenty feet behind him, so he now stood silhouetted in a ghostly glow.

'Would you be so kind as to let me pass, sir?' asked the old women politely.

Hook paused for a second, then in an eerie voice said, 'Hello, Mary . . .'

Startled, she looked up at the towering man and squinted her tired eyes, but couldn't see his face.

'How do you know my name? Do I know you, sir?'

'Oh, I know you, Mary. And you'll soon know me. All of London will soon know me.'

Slowly and with theatrical effect, he let his left arm, with the hook now attached to his stump, appear from under his long jacket sleeve. He brought it up to Mary's eyeline and held it menacingly in front of her face. The metal glistened in the light from the lamp at the end of the alley.

Mary gasped. She'd never seen such a sight.

'The devil!' she spluttered. 'You're the devil,' her voice trembling with fear. 'God help me,' and with that, unable to even look at him, Mary, as fast as her old legs could manage, scurried off back the way she'd come, while Hook bellowed out a deep belly laugh that chilled the very blood in her veins.

Mary Morgan was in no doubt that she had seen the devil that night. 'He wore a black coat, he did . . . I never saw his face, but he's the devil all right. And he doesn't have a cloven foot, he has a metal hook for a hand.'

Mary never wavered from her story and passed it down through the generations, to her children, grandchildren and even great-grandchildren. She went to her grave at the ripe old age of ninety-six, still claiming that she had come face to face with the devil himself. 'The devil exists, and I've seen him.'

Mary's reaction intrigued Hook. He'd meant it as pure mischief, to scare someone and give himself a laugh. But that woman wasn't merely scared. She was terrified out of her wits.

He may not have the magic the other inhabitants of Neverland had, but Hook now saw an opportunity to create his own brand of magic. Black magic, on the streets of London. He tucked the thought away in the back of his mind and continued walking.

* * *

It had been three days since his brief chat with the Darling family's neighbour. Hook had carefully staked out the house, observing its comings and goings. No one looking like Peter came in or out on day two, but on the Saturday morning, out strolled a boy . . .

Hiding behind a tree across the street, Hook studied him. He looked more grown-up than Pan. He wore normal, civilised clothes. Could it possibly be him? Hook followed the boy along the pavement at a discreet distance.

At the end of the road, the boy suddenly stopped. He looked right and left, then right again, and once over his right shoulder to check the junction. And as he did, Hook caught sight of his face. There was no doubt: this boy was Peter Pan.

Hook's heart thumped in his chest and it took all the self-discipline he could muster to stop himself from attaching his hook to his arm and ripping Pan's heart out there and then.

As if able to read his mind, Tink shouted in his ear, 'Bad form, Hook. Bad form!'

Hook took a deep breath, stayed put and let Pan go on his way. But he never once took his eyes off the boy as he declared, 'It's time for us to meet again, Pan. It's time . . .'

CHAPTER 23

Tink and Hook agreed a plan. They decided not to confront Peter in or around the Darling family home – too many opportunities for things to go wrong. Needing to pick their moment wisely, they decided their best bet was during one of Peter and Wendy's walks in Kensington Gardens. They chose a Sunday, it would be quieter then. Also, Mrs Darling would be home cooking the Sunday roast and Mr Darling off to buy the papers. No other family members around. Perfect timing indeed.

The plan was that Tink, depending on the circumstances, would distract Wendy, and anyone else who happened to be close by. She'd been experimenting with a spell to make Wendy temporarily fall asleep, giving them just enough time to confront Peter.

Hook would approach Peter first, followed by Tink, so that Pan would know he wasn't seeing things. With the proof that Hook was alive, Pan would have every reason to return to Neverland, then Tink would immediately whisk them both back home. A perfect plan, they both agreed.

'But what about Wendy?' Tink asked. 'We can't leave her asleep in a park.'

Hook shrugged, 'Not my concern. And I'm surprised to hear you care. She's the one who took Pan from us, after all.'

Hook was right – but still, Tink had no desire to put Wendy in harm's way. So she decided that once Hook and Peter were safely back to Neverland, she'd stay with Wendy until she woke up, and explain everything to her.

* * *

Perched high in a cherry tree across the street, Tink had been monitoring the Darling household from just after dawn. Mr Darling had left the house at nine in the morning and returned twenty minutes later carrying an armful of Sunday newspapers, but there was no sign of Peter yet.

Feeling frustrated, she considered flying in through a window and confronting him there and then. But she reluctantly stuck to the plan she'd agreed with Hook. Tink sat for another forty long minutes until the black front door opened and out stepped Wendy – and directly behind her, Peter.

'What is he wearing?' said Tink to herself as she shook her head at the oblivious boy. 'He looks so normal, so boring.'

Peter and Wendy strolled along the garden path and through the gate, turned left and headed down the street. Tink discreetly followed them for a good thirty minutes until they walked in through a black iron gate and into Kensington Gardens.

As fast as her tiny wings would carry her, she flew off to get Hook. They returned by horse and carriage taxi to the same spot, only thirty minutes later.

Excited that he was finally getting the chance to come face to face with Pan, Hook not only paid the driver without haggling, but even tipped him, and handsomely at that.

'Thanks guv'nor!' exclaimed the delighted cabbie. 'Have a good day, sir!'

'Oh I will, I will,' said Hook with a glint in his eye that made the cab driver suddenly feel nervous.

'Right, Miss Bell,' Hook declared to Tink, now in full fairy form. 'The moment of truth has finally arrived.' And with that, they entered the park.

* * *

It only took Hook and Tink a few minutes to spot Pan standing in the middle of a clump of bushes.

As luck would have it, Wendy was on a nearby pathway, twenty feet away, busy talking with a young woman rocking a pram.

'We're never going to get another chance like this, Hook. Come on, it's now or never. And remember, we're here to convince Pan to return to Neverland. And you agreed . . . no fighting.'

'Yes, yes!' Hook replied, increasingly annoyed at being told what to do. He took a deep breath, cleared his throat and walked towards Pan. Standing behind him, in a totally calm but classic Captain Hook voice he said, 'Hello, Pan . . . remember me?' He waited for Peter to turn around and see him.

Nothing. No reaction. Pan didn't even move.

He cleared his throat again, louder this time.

'Didn't you hear me, boy? Don't you recognise this voice? Don't you dare ignore me. Bad form Pan, bad form!'

Again, nothing.

'He's playing games. Insolent boy.'

Now sounding as if he wanted to kill him on the spot, Hook sneered through gritted teeth, 'And you thought I was dead. Well I'm not, I'm here, I'm back! Turn around and face Captain James Hook.'

Nothing. Pan just kept on inspecting the greenery in front of him.

'Let me try,' said Tink, 'He'll remember me. Peter, it's me. It's your old pal Tink,' she said, right in front of his face.

Nothing.

She waved her arms, blew raspberries. Nothing. She lifted his outer ear and screamed, 'Peter, it's me! It's Tinkerbell!'

Nothing. Tink flew back to Hook's shoulder. 'He can't see us. He can't even hear us.'

'But how is that possible? What's wrong with that boy? Is he suffering from amnesia? I'll soon shake him out of this.'

Hook pulled off his fake hand, replaced it with his hook and marched towards Peter. He carefully placed it around Pan's shoulder and whipped him round. They were now face to face.

Peter could see nothing. It was as if a freak gust of wind had just turned him round. He'd *felt* something . . . something strange, but he had no idea what it was.

Hook, who was now within inches of Pan's face, held up his hook and drifted it back and forth in front of his eyes – a move always guaranteed to put the fear of death into any boy.

Nothing. Pan just looked right through Hook. Suddenly Hook felt a pull on his jacket lapel as Tink pulled him back a few feet. She'd come to the only conclusion she could. 'He doesn't believe anymore.'

'What do you mean, he doesn't believe anymore? Believe in what?'

'Us. Everything. Himself. He's forgotten who he is. He's forgotten all about Neverland.'

'Impossible.'

'No. It's true. You waved the hook in front of his eyes. He's not playing games, he can't see you. We're invisible to him, because he doesn't believe anymore. He doesn't believe in you; he doesn't believe in fairies. He can't see or hear us because he's not a child anymore.'

'But other people can see me. That annoying neighbour of the Darling family for a start.'

'That's because you were not the real you when you spoke to him. You were in disguise. Pan only knows you as Hook. And sadly he doesn't believe anymore, so he can't see you.'

'Peter? Peter!' Wendy was calling him and he snapped out of his daze.

'Yes?'

'Are you OK? You seem distracted.'

He smiled, 'I'm fine, just strange thoughts, a strange feeling . . . it's nothing really.'

Peter took one last glance around him, before shouting over, 'I'm coming, Wendy!'

Hook and Tink watched as Pan ran over to Wendy. He kissed her on the cheek, linked his arm in hers and off they strolled.

Hook stood rooted to the spot, speechless. Tink sat on his left shoulder and cried.

CHAPTER 24

Hook was totally deflated. He'd just seen it with his own eyes: Peter Pan was no more. The mischievous boy he longed to fight and one day finally defeat was gone. Peter Pan had grown up. Hook sat slumped on a bench in Kensington Gardens.

'C'mon Hook, let's get out of here, it's horrible, too wet and cold,' said Tink.

'To where?' Hook replied, not caring.

'Neverland, of course,' said Tink surprised.

'What's the point?'

Tink tried to convince Hook, but even her heart wasn't in it. He'd heard enough and cut her off in mid-sentence.

'Miss Bell, please, stop. I'm not coming back to Neverland.'

'But where will you go?'

'I'm staying here.'

'Here? In this awful, noisy, busy, grown-up place?'

'Neverland is not for me anymore. I'm staying here.'

'But what will I tell the Lost Boys and the pirates?'

'Tell them what you wish, I couldn't care less. It's over, can't you see that? Your precious Peter Pan has left you, too.'

These words stung Tink, because she knew they were true.

'Well, I'm not coming back here,' she said with conviction. 'So you're on your own. You won't be able to just summon me to magic you back if you change your mind. Once I'm gone, I'm gone.'

'I understand.'

'Suit yourself. Well, there's no point in me hanging around here, Hook, I'm off to Neverland, to tell the Lost Boys.'

She looked at Hook one last time, and even felt sorry for him.

'Goodbye Hook . . .'

'Goodbye, Miss Bell . . .' and with what bordered on actual kindness, he added, 'Take care of yourself . . .'

'You too . . .' And with that, Tink vanished.

Hook sat in silence and contemplated his future. After an hour, he concluded that maybe, just maybe, it wasn't so bleak after all. *I'm sure this big city has many opportunities for someone of my talents*, he thought, as he rubbed at the stump on the end of his arm. *Maybe even my old hook needs to be used again. Yes, that could cause some mischief on the streets.* He got up off the bench and walked in the general direction of Piccadilly Circus.

As he walked, he cast his mind back to the incident with that woman, what was her name again? Ah yes, Mary. He remembered the terror in her eyes at seeing his hook. She had genuinely believed that he was the devil. 'I could create havoc here,' he said to himself with a smile.

* * *

Hook spent three nights after the Kensington Gardens incident getting very drunk on rum in the Lamb and Flag.

He cursed Peter Pan, cursed him numerous times. Those sitting nearby simply ignored him – just another crazy old drunk. But getting drunk and letting go of past frustrations had been excellent therapy for Hook, and by day four, he claimed to have gotten Pan out of his system.

'Things happen for a reason,' he now told himself. 'Hang Peter Pan and Neverland. That's history. It's time for me to look to my future. Yes, it's time to introduce London to James Hook.'

A contented smile spread over his face. And for the first time in days, Hook now walked with real purpose. Back straight and head held high.

With a new cane he'd stolen from a stall in Petticoat Lane market, Hook strode elegantly along the Strand. Since Tinkerbell had left, he'd spent a couple of days picking pockets. He'd come away with wallets, handkerchiefs, even jewellery. It was a good start, and enabled him to pay his rent and feed himself. But Hook had no desire to be a petty thief long term – he had much bigger plans for his future.

Suddenly he stopped. Something had caught his eye. Him. His own name.

'It can't be . . .'

Hook turned to his left, walked back six paces and looked at the poster, which he read with astonishment.

A new and exciting play by Mr J. M. Barrie.

Lose yourself in the most wondrous, magical place on earth. A land of Indians and mermaids. Meet the boys who live there and their child leader, Peter Pan, the boy who never grew up. Come face to face with the scary pirate Captain Hook!

For children and all those young at heart.

**The Garrick Theatre, Saturday 7 p.m.
for one night only:**

'Adventures in Neverland'

* * *

Hook had spent the past hour in a bookshop off Charing Cross Road, enquiring who this J. M. Barrie was. The elderly gentleman owner directed his customer to a rack of books and plays by Mr Barrie.

'Is this Mr Barrie any good?'

'Oh, Mr Barrie is wonderful, sir. He is my favourite author. And he has a new play on this weekend. It's about a mythical island with magic and pirates. Are you going to see it? I am, and I'm sure it will be splendid, just like all of Mr Barrie's plays.'

'I haven't decided yet, but maybe I will,' Hook replied.

Of course he'd go, his pride wouldn't allow him not to. As Hook flicked through a copy of Barrie's plays, his mind drifted off . . . *A play about me? How fitting. Oh, how the audience will be in awe at the sight of the world's greatest ever pirate and how he rules over Neverland. A play about me, with London's finest in the audience. This will help to put me on the map.*

Hook thanked the owner of the bookshop and was in such a good mood now he saw himself as an up-and-coming star of the London stage, that he stole nothing. He actually paid for a copy of one of Mr Barrie's books. Of course, he'd stolen the money in the first place, but credit where credit's due.

Hook left the shop carrying his J. M. Barrie book, which had been wrapped in brown paper. He was pleased with what he'd learned. There was no doubt his confidence was growing by the day.

However, that confidence would soon turn out to be misplaced. Very misplaced indeed.

CHAPTER 25

The Garrick Theatre was one of London's finest, and normally impossible to get for a one-night performance – but there had been a cancellation two months back, and being on good terms with the management, Mr Barrie was offered the whole week's slot at a much reduced cost.

Rehearsals had gone well, the cast had worked hard, and splendid sets resembling Neverland had been built.

Securing the theatre for an entire week meant the cast could rehearse on stage every day. Mr Whitmore, the manager of the Garrick, had watched the final two days of rehearsals with interest. He liked to consider himself an open-minded man, and while he'd enjoyed watching the play, he was concerned he'd made a grave mistake by letting it be staged in his highly respected theatre.

What would London's finest theatre-going crowd make of this? Pirates and mermaids, fantasy islands, a dog as a nanny, not to mention a boy who never grew up and could fly?

Whitmore knew his business. London's theatre crowd could be an extremely difficult lot to please.

The single-night performance was a sell-out. Only days ago, a mysterious lone gentleman had even paid the full asking price for the royal box. A full house – every theatre manager's dream.

As the crew put the finishing touches to the set and for the umpteenth time made sure the wires were secure for the flying scene, author and theatre manager sat in the front row of the stalls in the empty auditorium.

'Looking good, James, really good. It's a gamble though, I'll tell you that.'

'How do you mean?' asked Barrie.

'Well, it's not really a play for adults, and not even children. It's for neither, or both. You've either got an enormous success on your hands, or a major flop. And if it's a flop, you've ruined your reputation, you realise that don't you?'

'Yes . . . but it's a chance I'm willing to take.'

'But not only that, my friend, if you flop, you take my reputation down with you.'

Barrie had to admit to himself, he'd never considered that. It was a valid point.

'Don't worry, Gerald. I believe in this story, I really believe in it.'

'It's not what *you* believe James, it's what the eight hundred good people of London in my audience believe that matters.' He gave his friend a wry smile, and got up to leave, before adding, 'And I guess we'll find out Saturday won't we?'

He patted Barrie on the shoulder, 'Good luck, old boy. I think we may just need it.'

* * *

Back in Neverland, Tink couldn't get over the loss of Peter.

At first she was angry at him, angry at Wendy, angry with the world. Eventually her anger subsided, but life just wasn't the same, and never would be again.

One day, when visiting Migizi, she blurted out her feelings of being lost without Peter Pan. He sympathised with her, but then said, 'He has made his choice.'

'Not the answer I wanted to hear,' grumbled Tink.

He understood, but added, 'We must respect each other's decisions. Have you not considered that Pan may be happy where he is now? Is that not what you should want? For him to be happy?'

Tink was torn. Torn between the sense Migizi had just spoken and her own inner thoughts.

'But what if he's not happy? What if he wants to come back, but can't?'

Migizi took a long pause to think. 'If it will put your mind at rest, there's only one way to find out . . .'

Tink let the words sink in, thanked the chief for his wise thoughts and flew off in a hurry. It didn't take her long to make her mind up. She'd go to London for one last time. She wouldn't plead with Peter though – that was pointless, since he couldn't even see her. Tink only wanted to see how he was, and make sure he was happy. If she saw he was truly happy, she decided she'd leave him be, and that would be the end of that.

She didn't tell the Lost Boys, didn't even tell Ilba. She left for London early the next morning.

* * *

Mr Darling, immensely proud with his daughter Wendy on his arm, stepped into the plush foyer of the Garrick Theatre on opening night. Mrs Darling was having one of her famous migraines that day, so had decided not to go with them.

'This is so exciting!' said Wendy, sounding younger than her years. 'To think, we're going to watch the play that Mr Barrie wrote about my stories of Neverland.'

Mr Darling beamed at his daughter. 'I'm so proud of you, Wendy. I hope you'll go on to write your own stories one day, maybe even a play, too.'

'I'd like nothing more, Father.'

'But remember my dear, no one must ever know that – well I find it hard to say, even to this day – but no one must know that Neverland is real and that you actually went there.'

Wendy chuckled. 'They'd never believe me anyway. Even Mr Barrie thinks I made it up or dreamt it, and that's the way it shall stay.'

Suddenly Mr Darling glanced around, and turned back to his daughter. 'But where's Peter? He got out of the carriage with us. He hasn't changed his mind, has he?'

'No, he's gone backstage. Mr Barrie promised him he could go and view the sets. He's never been inside a theatre before.'

Mr Darling was concerned. 'Are you sure he's OK with this? I mean, seeing his life – his old life – on stage?'

'I think so, Father.'

But Mr Darling wasn't so sure. 'Peter has made so much progress . . . I wouldn't want this play to drag him backwards.'

'To be honest, I feel it will help him. He seems to have accepted once and for all that with Hook gone forever, it's time for him to grow up and move on with his life. And hopefully that will be here, with me – with us,

I mean,' she quickly added, feeling a little embarrassed.

Mr Darling kissed his daughter on the forehead. 'I'm going into the bar – a small celebratory drink to toast the evening. You don't mind do you?'

'Not at all, Father. I'm going to buy a programme. I'll meet you later.'

* * *

Tink had arrived in London the very day of the performance, which of course she knew nothing of. She flew to the Darling family home, but saw no sign of Peter through the nursery window. She flew to Kensington Gardens, but again no sign.

After spending the entire afternoon flying over London without any luck, she was ready to give up. Maybe Peter had already moved away to another city?

'This is pointless. I'm going home,' she grumbled. Perched high on Nelson's Column, she'd twice had to shoo off a gang of large pigeons, who seemed to think she was a tasty insect to be gobbled up. 'Beat it!' she chastised them.

Tink flew over Trafalgar Square, turned left, and after a few hundred feet, spotted a large crowd of people outside a grand-looking building. For no reason other than curiosity, she swooped down to see what was happening. Seconds later, she landed on the Garrick Theatre. Staring at the hundreds of humans going in through the front door, she wondered what could be inside such a building.

She flew down to street level to get a better view and spotted a poster facing out from the glass windows.

A new and exciting play by Mr J. M. Barrie.

Lose yourself in the most wondrous, magical place on earth. A land of Indians and mermaids. Meet the boys who live there and their child leader, Peter Pan, the boy who never grew up. Come face to face with the scary pirate Captain Hook!

For children and all those young at heart.

The Garrick Theatre, Saturday 7 p.m. for one night only:

'Adventures in Neverland'

Tink couldn't believe what she'd just read. She sat on the branch of a tree opposite the theatre for a good ten minutes, trying to make sense of it all. Suddenly, she noticed that the throng of humans had gone inside, and a man in a black suit and tie was about to close the front door.

'I've just got to see this,' she said, and flew towards the door, which was only inches from being closed.

'Pesky fly!' the official-looking man grunted, and swatted at Tink as she flew past him and into the building. He closed the door. The Garrick had a full house, plus one little fairy.

Tink flew through the foyer, upstairs and into the auditorium.

Having never been in a theatre before, she was mesmerised by the lights, the stage and, well, everything. People in their hundreds, all dressed in their finest clothes, took to their seats.

She flitted around, taking in her surroundings, before choosing herself a comfy spot atop a huge stage spotlight, hanging on a wire under the royal box. She settled down and waited for the performance to start.

* * *

Hook stood at the dress circle bar. A few feet away, Mr Darling stood at the same bar. Neither of them paid any heed to the other, both men lost in their own thoughts, quietly waiting to be served. But if you'd been a casual observer that night, you might have spotted some intriguing similarities between the two strangers. They didn't look alike, but both men gently tugged at the bottom of their shirt sleeve, making sure it sat just an inch under the jacket line. Both flicked a piece of fluff, or imaginary fluff, off their left jacket lapel, and finally, when a barman appeared in front of them, both cleared their throats in the same manner and at exactly the same time.

'Yes, gents, who's first?' said the cheery barman.

'This gentleman,' replied Mr Darling.

Hook nodded his thanks and ordered a large glass of rum.

'Something to keep out the cold?' asked Mr Darling, trying to make polite conversation.

'Something like that,' Hook replied. And with that, he took his drink and removed himself to a table in the far corner.

'And you sir?' the barman asked Mr Darling.

'A port and lemon, please.'

As Mr Darling sipped his port and lemon, he turned to face the area behind him. A pre-theatre drink was always a joy before a performance. His eye went to the man who'd been standing next to him a moment or so ago. Did he know him? He couldn't recall him, but there was something about him – something not exactly familiar, but that held his attention. He watched the man drinking his rum.

Mr Darling took his own drink, and walked towards him. He coughed, to alert the man to his presence, then asked politely, 'Excuse me, and forgive me for intruding, but . . . do I know you, sir?'

Hook looked up from the small table where he was reading the programme he'd expertly snatched from the lady in the foyer and replied, 'No, I don't think so.'

'Possibly I've seen you at the bank on the Strand where I work . . .'

'I doubt that, sir. I don't trust banks, and I don't trust bankers. Never have done.'

Always the gentleman, Mr Darling, replied, 'Oh, I see . . . but I'm sure I've seen you or know of you. May I ask your name sir?'

Damn, who was this man? An off-duty police officer? Hook kept calm as he looked up at the annoying man and gave him a false name, the first that came into his head.

'Harold James.'

'Are you from London, Mr James?'

'Originally, yes, but I moved away a long time ago. Back in town for . . . well, business.'

'Theatre business?'

Hook was getting fed up with this, 'Something like that.'

Knowing that this was about as far as polite conversation with a stranger should go, Mr Darling said, 'Well, I've taken up enough of your time. Please forgive my intrusion. Enjoy your evening, Mr James.'

'And you,' Hook replied.

Mr Darling walked off, coming to the conclusion he'd made a mistake. London was full of people, and everyone has a double, they say.

Yet something niggled him. He couldn't put his finger on it. Something deep inside was trying very hard to tell him, *you know this man.*

Ladies and gentlemen, this evening's performance will begin in exactly three minutes, declared the voice of an usher who had entered the bar, before continuing, *Please take your seats for the performance. Thank you.*

'Father, the play is about to begin!' An excited Wendy had appeared at his side. 'Peter's already in his seat. Come on, Father, we don't want to miss the start.'

'Hmm?' he replied absently, unable to take his eyes off the man still sitting in the corner.

'Are you all right?'

'Yes, yes, I'm fine.' He looked back over at Hook one last time, 'I thought I saw someone . . . someone I should know.'

'Who, Father?'

Mr Darling gave her a puzzled look, before saying, 'I must be mistaken, come, let's take our seats.'

Hook, paying no attention to the Darling conversation twenty feet away, unconsciously fiddled with the locket round his neck one last time, gulped the remains of his rum and left the bar to take his seat in the royal box.

Wendy and Mr Darling joined Peter, already sitting in his seat in the middle of the fourth row of the dress circle.

'Are you excited, Peter?' asked Wendy.

'Yes, looking forward to it. But it does feel strange.'

'It must be. But remember,' she said as she took his hand, 'it's all in the past now, and after tonight we move on with our lives.'

Peter nodded and smiled. She was the kindest, most gentle and caring person he had ever known. Yet as he looked out over the auditorium, there was still a hint of that far-off sad look in his eye. And it didn't go unnoticed by Wendy.

Tink, still sat atop her spotlight, had not seen Peter and Wendy take their seats, as there were hundreds of people in the building now. She did occasionally look around, but just as her eyes fell on the spot where Peter sat, the theatre lights dimmed and suddenly they were in darkness.

The curtain lifted, bringing the nursery in the Darling family home to life.

'I won't go to bed Nana, I won't, I won't, I won't!' cried the young actor playing Michael.

Nana woofed her displeasure and the actor inside the dog costume chased Michael and John around the stage on all fours. The comedy continued for the next five minutes as Nana tried in vain to get the boys to take a bath.

Mr Barrie knew that first impressions were vital. Nervously he took in his surroundings. The big fluffy dog in charge of everyone had totally captivated the audience . . . the adults were smiling and the children laughing.

'Off to a good start,' he said to himself. He looked over at Mr Whitmore. Both men shared a look of *so far so good*.

On stage, Tinkerbell never appeared as a fairy: that would have been impossible. Instead, she was cast as the sound of a bell, rung off-stage by a member of the crew. Not being seen on stage didn't bother Tink one bit; she just sat back on her spotlight and took in the spectacle. She was enjoying herself immensely.

CHAPTER 26

The opening scenes of the play, with the Darling family in London and Peter Pan appearing and whisking Wendy off to Neverland, didn't bother Hook. But as soon as Scene Four began, it became obvious that this was not going to be a pro-Hook play. His earlier dreams of a performance showering him in glory evaporated.

The actor who played him wasn't so terrible to start. In fact, there was hope when he told the audience that he ruled Neverland and wanted to kill Peter Pan – but the dialogue between him and Smee left a lot to be desired. Hook grumbled to himself as the actor droned on and on. He had no fear factor – he was an idiot! Hook flicked through his programme. 'Mr J. M. Barrie, is it? Well, Mr Barrie, you and I are going to meet again, and it won't be pleasant for you.'

Soon, Hook's grumbling turned to anger. Scene after scene portrayed Hook as a fool, incapable of beating Pan and the Lost Boys. He was even shown being scared of the mermaids. But most displeasing for him was the audience's reaction. As the actor playing Hook walked around the set, which now resembled the *Jolly Roger*, the real Hook sat aghast as the audience laughed at his incompetence. He had become a figure of ridicule.

'How dare they laugh at me,' Hook growled quietly to himself as he peered out at the audience. 'I am the most respected and feared pirate that has ever lived. Who is this fool on the stage? Certainly not the great Captain James Hook.'

The play continued, as Hook sat in the royal box getting more and more frustrated. Then came the final straw. The actor who played Hook was in the middle of a sword fight with Peter Pan. Pan had jumped up and pulled Hook's ridiculous-looking hat down over his ears and face, which caused Hook to wander around the stage screaming out to Smee that he was scared of the dark, while the Lost Boys took it in turns to whack his bottom with sticks. The adults in the audience laughed. As for the children, they were in hysterics.

Enough was enough. Hook's frustration finally boiled over and he could take no more. Without even thinking, he rose out of his seat, put his hands firmly on the ledge in front of him and bellowed, 'Stop laughing at this nonsense! How dare you! Ignore this act of treachery, for I am the real Captain James Hook!'

Tink sat bolt upright, stared at the shouting man, and nearly fell off her spotlight. 'Hook? What on earth is he doing here? What's going on?'

The cast on stage froze, dumbstruck, as the entire audience turned and stared at the man in the royal box. Total silence in the theatre. The audience's faces were a mix of impressed, unsure and uneasy. What would happen next in this extremely unusual play?

'Don't believe me? Don't believe that I am the real Hook? Watch this.'

Hook pulled off his fake hand and flung it towards the stage where it landed with a thump. The audience gasped, but nothing prepared them for what he did next. From inside a shoulder bag he took out his hook, and firmly screwed it into place on the stump at the end of his arm. With a steely glare, he held it up for the audience to see.

Hook looked down at the stage. Too far to jump – he'd break his neck. Suddenly he spotted the thick red velvet curtain that hung at the side of the stage, almost within reaching distance. He knew what to do – he just hoped it would take his weight. To the fascination of the audience, now on the edges of their seats, Hook stood up somewhat precariously on the ledge of the royal box and propelled himself through the air towards the velvet curtain, with his hook outstretched. On contact with the curtain, he sank his hook into it, using it to slow his fall to the stage. Hook slowly descended onto the very edge of the stage as the cloth gave a harsh tearing sound. The audience gasped again, unable to take their eyes off him.

Hook strutted towards centre stage and for the first time in his life experienced applause. The audience were clapping him. People loved him . . . and Hook loved that feeling. He looked out towards the audience – his audience – and revelled in it.

Tink sat glued to her spot. *What is he up to?* Should she intervene? She didn't know. She scanned her eyes over the audience below in the stalls, but she couldn't make anyone out in the dark.

Eventually, she spotted Wendy, and next to her, Peter Pan. Tink's heart raced with joy, but fear quickly overwhelmed her.

Hook.

'I have a bad feeling about this,' Tink muttered to herself.

The stunned cast, having no clue what was going on, reacted in different ways. The poor actor playing Hook looked towards the stage manager and mouthed, 'What am I supposed to do?'

The stage manager, unseen to the audience, and as surprised as everyone else, shook his head and shrugged. Three cast members left the stage at once. Two hid behind props, while the others stood rooted to the spot. But with encouragement from the stage manager, who was now fearful that this man who had climbed onto the stage might be a lunatic, the entire cast was soon coaxed off. This left the real Hook with an empty stage, entirely to himself.

No one knew what was going on, especially not Mr J. M. Barrie, sitting along the row from Wendy in the dress circle.

The only person in the audience who had any clue, apart from Tink, was Wendy. From the moment Hook had shouted from the royal box, she knew it was him.

But how could it be? He was supposed to be dead. What on earth was he doing in London? Wendy suddenly realised, and feared the worst. He had come looking for Peter Pan.

She turned to Peter with her mouth hanging open. She tried to speak but no words came out. Peter just looked confused.

Suddenly Tink appeared at Peter's left ear.

'Snap out of it. C'mon, Hook's here – you've got to stand up to him!'

But still Peter couldn't see her – he didn't even hear her words, only the faint ringing of a bell. He knew that sound, but couldn't place it . . . he felt dazed and confused.

Tink flew around Peter's head, speaking into his left and right ears, trying in vain to rouse him.

'C'mon Peter, snap out of it!' No response, nothing.

'Hook's back, Peter, and he's come for you. Are you going to let Hook win? You've got to wake up, Peter.'

Suddenly Tink noticed a flicker in Peter's eyes. She rapped her tiny knuckles against his head. 'I know you're in there, Peter Pan!'

Time to try some telepathy, thought Tink, and she summoned up mental images of the Lost Boys. Soon the faces of Peter's friends appeared before him. Tootles, Nibs, the twins and all the rest. They smiled lovingly at him, and one by one, repeated the following line.

'Come back to us Peter Pan, come back to us . . .'

Peter began to look as if he were waking up from a coma.

Tink, flitting from ear to ear, kept whispering, 'Come on Peter, believe, just believe.'

Tink then conjured up images of the mermaids. They didn't speak, but swam around in front of Peter's gaze. So close that Peter felt as if they were swimming inside his very own eyes. He smiled a drunken smile at the wonderful sight of them.

It was working, but Tink worried the moment might soon pass. When Hook left the stage or someone threw him out, her last chance to bring Pan to his senses would be gone, forever.

She turned to face Wendy, sitting to Peter's left, and carefully tapped her on the nose with her wand, thus allowing Wendy to see her. Wendy blinked and looked startled as Tink appeared before her eyes.

Now these two, as you already know, had never had

the closest of relationships, yet Wendy knew that Tink cared deeply for Peter. It took little explanation for Wendy to understand.

Hovering right in front of Wendy's face, Tink was frantic as she pleaded, 'I need your help, Wendy, you know he's the real Hook, right? And he's here!' She jabbed a small fairy finger towards the stage below. 'Hook's back, Wendy, and we need Peter back. Now!'

Wendy looked at Tink, and then at Peter, who still seemed to be in a daze. She glanced at the stage and saw Hook ranting and raving at the mesmerised audience, who were hanging on his every word. Torn between helping Tink and wanting to keep Peter with her in London, she knew she had to help. Tink pleaded again, but ironically it was Hook who finally tipped the balance in her favour.

He bellowed out from the centre of the stage, 'Peter Pan is no hero, he is a coward! The boy who never grew up? Pah! He left Neverland. Why? Because he couldn't face me anymore. He lost his nerve and ran away with his tail between his legs. And then, ladies and gentlemen of the audience, Peter Pan grew up!'

The audience, still believing it all part of the play, started to believe Hook. As for poor Mr Barrie, well, he was at a total loss. 'This wasn't in my script . . .' he muttered, as Hook finished his triumphant rant.

In full flow, Hook continued, 'Peter Pan failed, he ran away from Neverland and grew up. So I have finally won. I have beaten Peter Pan! I have won!'

Wendy could not let that happen. She nodded at Tink, then turned to Peter, took his hand and whispered in his ear, 'You are the real Peter Pan . . . the boy who never grew up . . . I believe in you, Peter Pan, I believe in you!'

Tink was now hovering directly in front of Peter's face, inches from his nose. She looked directly into his eyes and kept repeating over and over, 'You are the real Peter Pan, come back to us Peter, please come back . . .'

Slowly but surely, something happened, as Peter saw small pulsating lights in front of his eyes. He tried to blink them away, but they grew stronger and stronger as Tink kept repeating, 'Come back to us Peter, come back . . .'

As if he were being hypnotised he focused on the dancing lights and suddenly they merged into a solid shape. Blurry at first, they then transformed into a real live fairy.

'Tink?'

Tinkerbell nearly exploded with joy and started laughing and clapping. 'Can you see me, Peter? Can you?'

'Yes . . . I can . . . see you.' But he still looked dazed.

Tink kept at him. 'Hook's back, Peter, he's not dead, he's here and you've got to stand up to him.'

Tink looked at Peter, willing him with all her might.

'Are you going to let Hook win? You can't, Peter, you've got to fight him. Come on, you're Peter Pan. Say it. You're Peter Pan, SAY IT!'

Unsure at first, he said 'I'm Peter Pan . . .' But then with more conviction, 'I'm Peter Pan!' The look in his eyes had returned, that adventurous, thrilling look.

'Say it louder Peter, say it louder and tell the world!' bellowed Tink.

Peter stood bolt up right and with all the power he could muster shouted out to a startled audience, 'I am Peter Pan and I believe in fairies!'

And as soon as those words left Pan's lips, a stream of hot energy gushed through his entire body, which lifted him up off the ground. He hovered in the air, ten feet above the audience.

Mr Darling, even though he knew the reality of Peter Pan, was as dumbstruck as everyone else.

'Oh dear . . . what happens now, Wendy?' he asked.

'I have no idea,' she replied.

Meanwhile, gasps from the audience filled the air.

'Good heavens!'

'Well, I'll be . . .'

'Oh my!'

Peter had never felt so alive. As he hovered in mid-air, he looked at Wendy and the stunned audience. He grinned and winked at Wendy, before taking off and flying all over the theatre. The audience was in total awe, and as Peter flew around the auditorium, up and around over and over like a bird suddenly released from a small cage for the first time, they got to their feet and applauded.

'I can't see the wires, where are the wires?'

'How does he do that?'

'Well Mr Barrie, you've certainly outdone yourself this time,' said a voice from behind him.

And another, 'Splendid, splendid!'

'First class Mr Barrie, how did you manage to make that boy fly? I can't even see the wires.'

Mr Barrie, for the first time in his life, was at a loss for words. He could only nod in embarrassment, while saying under his breath, 'No, neither can I.'

As he sat in his seat, he leaned forward and looked across at Wendy. His face said inquisitively, *Well?*

Wendy smiled nervously and shrugged as if to say, *I'll explain everything later.*

On stage, Hook stood glued to the spot. Stunned at first, he now had a wicked grin on his face.

'He lives! Pan lives!'

However, not everyone was impressed.

'Good lord, what is this sorcery?' spluttered an annoyed elderly gentleman in the audience as he watched Peter Pan flying around. 'There's black magic at work here, maybe even the devil himself. I will have to inform the bishop. Come Margery, we are leaving, at once!'

And with that, Lord Hoppington guided his poor lady wife out of their seats and marched her out of the building. Which was a shame, as Lady Hoppington had been rather enjoying herself.

It went down in theatre history as the most spectacular live performance ever seen on a London stage. No one who was present that night would ever forget it. In London's more fashionable private clubs, the tale of the 'real' Peter Pan flying around the auditorium with no wires or props is still talked about to this very day.

Peter Pan came to a stop and hovered over the stage. With ease and a big grin on his face, he floated down and landed with both feet firmly on stage, a mere ten feet from where Hook stood.

'Hello, old man . . .'

CHAPTER 27

The audience sat speechless. *This play by Mr Barrie just kept on getting better and better.*

Mr Barrie had moved himself into Peter's seat, next to Wendy. He turned to face her and whispered, 'It's real isn't it, Wendy? You didn't have dreams, these people are real. You've been to Neverland . . .'

Wendy nodded.

Mr Barrie let out a huge but near-silent breath. Even for a man who spent his entire life writing and living inside the heads of children, it was still hard to accept. But he had to – it was happening right in front of him, in the middle of his own play.

'What happens now? How does this end?' he asked Wendy.

'I don't really know . . . but I've got a feeling it won't be good. I've never seen Hook so determined.'

On stage, the old grudging respect between these two great foes was clear.

'Peter Pan. So, it appears that you can still fly. Which I presume means you didn't grow up after all. Good form Pan, good form.'

Hook then looked Peter up and down and belly-laughed at the clothes he was wearing. 'You look ridiculous Pan, like a mannequin I saw in a shop window in Harrods.'

The audience laughed, and Peter turned bright red. But he ignored the comment. 'And it appears that you came back from the dead, Hook. That croc not like the taste of you? No surprise there.'

Hook explained to Peter and the audience about the croc, although in his version he'd wrestled with it before tearing it in two. He mentioned the desert island where he said he'd planned his revenge. Of course he conveniently missed out the embarrassing stuff about being depressed, fat and bald, and having no teeth.

'I'm back, Pan. And I want you.' He said it with such menace, the audience believed he was one heck of an actor. 'And I aim to end this once and for all.'

'Suits me fine, old man.'

Captain James Hook's arm crept towards Pan, his hook glistening under the powerful theatre spotlights. He played with it, twisting it ever so slowly from side to side, never once taking his eyes off his foe. The audience were mesmerised, and even Peter swallowed once at the sight of that hook again. He could see Hook's eyes were burning coals – and with that momentary distraction, Hook let out an inhuman animal sound from somewhere deep inside him, and brought his hook slashing across the face of Peter Pan.

An inch closer and Peter would have lost an eye. As it was, the wound was only superficial, but still, blood did splatter onto the stage canvas. The audience were impressed beyond belief, though some of the smaller children started to cry.

'A fight to the death, Pan?' enquired Hook, now looking the stronger of the two.

'A fight to the death, Hook,' snarled Pan.

And with that, they started fighting – not with swords of course, as there weren't any. Hook had initially picked up a sword left abandoned on stage by one of the actors, but he soon realised it was a stage prop, made of wood. Peter didn't have his dagger either. So instead, Hook grabbed at any solid object he could grasp and swung it at Pan, who ducked, dived and flew around, mocking Hook. He even toppled pieces of the set onto him.

The on-stage fight got more violent, as Peter unscrewed an overhanging stage light and it dropped, just missing Hook's head. A horrified Wendy pleaded with Mr Barrie. 'You've got to do something, you've got to stop this, now!'

Mr Barrie left his seat and ran out of the dress circle as fast as he could. No one noticed though, they were totally fixated on the fight between Pan and Hook.

'Well, I've seen stage fighting before, but never so realistic as this,' announced an excited gentleman to his wife. She nodded enthusiastically, without once taking her eyes off the stage, and stuffing yet another chocolate into her mouth.

Mr Barrie made it backstage in record time. He was out of breath and nearly clattered into the stage manager, who was clearly not happy.

'This,' he said, pointing to the on-stage fight, which was getting more realistic by the second, 'is NOT in my script, Mr Barrie.'

Once Barrie had got his breath back, he replied, 'It's not in mine either.'

The stage manager did not know what to think.

'Curtain, Mr Knowles, curtain! Pull the curtain!' Mr Barrie said through gritted teeth.

'Yes, sir,' replied the stage manager, and with Peter and Hook now centre stage in a classic do-or-die moment, the curtain came down six feet in front of them.

It didn't just come down though, it came down with thunderous applause and a standing ovation from the totally enthralled audience.

What an end to the play.

While the applause was thundering around them, Wendy frantically whispered to Tink, 'Do something Tink, they can't fight here – do something or they'll kill each other!'

Tink understood, nodded, and vanished. Seconds later, she appeared behind the curtain, where Hook and Pan were still on stage.

Both of them were momentarily distracted, not sure what would happen next. Pan turned to Tink, and in that second of confusion, Hook saw his chance and swung his hook in Pan's direction. But Tink saw it, and flashed her little wand, which froze him in an instant. 'Bad form, Hook!' she added for good measure.

Before Pan could open his mouth, Tink froze him as well. She then flew back to Wendy, and explained what she'd done. She also admitted that her spell could only last a few minutes.

Backstage, Mr Whitmore the theatre manager marched up to Mr Barrie and was ready to explode, but then stood rooted to the spot as he heard the thunderous applause.

'I don't know what you did there, James, I really don't, but . . . well, it's worked.' He grabbed a megaphone from the stage manager, slipped in front of the curtain, cleared his throat and said in as calm a voice as he could, 'Ladies and gentlemen, that concludes this evening's performance. Please leave the theatre in an orderly fashion. Thank you.'

And with that, the audience, chattering like a flock of excited geese, left the auditorium.

'I think an explanation is in order, Wendy,' said Mr Darling.

'I, I . . . don't have one. Not yet, anyway. I'll try to sort it out.'

'That man – is it possible – I mean, is he the real Captain Hook, the one you met in Neverland?'

'I'm afraid so, Father.'

'But what on earth is he doing here in London? I can't believe it.'

'Neither can I.'

'And he's the same man I met in the bar, and I thought I knew him . . . and . . .'

'Father, please just go, I'll wait here for Peter and Mr Barrie and try to make sense of it.'

'But Hook is here – the real one, I mean. He's dangerous, Wendy, I can't leave you here with—'

'Father.' She placed her hand on his arm. 'No harm will come to me, not while Peter is here.'

Mr Darling reluctantly accepted that. 'But how will you get home?'

'Mr Barrie will make sure Peter and I get home. Don't worry.'

'If you're sure . . .' He wasn't convinced, but he trusted his daughter, and Mr Barrie. He wasn't so sure about Peter Pan anymore though.

'Yes, Father, and thank you.'

'One last thing, Wendy. Tell me, did I see it with my own eyes? Did Peter actually fly? I mean, really fly?'

'Yes, Father.' She didn't say it with excitement at such an amazing thing, though – but with a tinge of sadness, because it could only mean one thing. Peter, the boy she'd hoped had grown up, was Peter Pan once again.

* * *

'Everyone has left, Tinkerbell,' said Wendy, who was the only person left in the dress circle.

'And backstage too,' said Tink.

Suddenly they heard voices on stage.

'The frozen spell, it's breaking,' said Tink

'Take up the curtain, Tink.'

And with a single flash of her wand, the curtain rose, showing Hook and Peter on stage. As if they were waking from sleep, they both came to their senses, took in their surroundings and each other, and started to fight again.

Exasperated, Wendy stood with her hands firmly grasping the safety rail in front of her. Hook swung at Pan but Pan dodged the blow by flying through Hook's legs and swiftly kicking him up the backside.

'Enough!' shouted Wendy. 'Peter, enough. You can't fight here.'

Hook and Pan looked at each other like two scolded schoolboys. It was Hook who spoke first.

'Well, well. Wendy Moira Angela Darling, if I'm not mistaken. So glad you stayed, my dear, but a word of warning – there will be blood spilled here, and it won't be mine.' No sooner had the words left Hook's mouth than he lashed in Pan's direction with his hook – but Peter just laughed as he easily dodged it.

'Enough!' Wendy repeated, but this time with anger. 'I want no more of this. You've just terrorised an entire London theatre, but it doesn't seem to bother either of you. Why must there always be fighting? Can't you learn to live with each other? Have neither of you learned anything? Peter, you were miserable when you thought Hook dead. And as for you Hook, Tinkerbell told me that you were miserable when Peter had left Neverland and grown up. Now you want to kill each other? It's senseless. Don't you see? You both need each other.' She sounded far more mature than her years.

Wendy let her powerful words hang in the air for a few seconds before adding, 'Let me ask you this. If one of you does manage to kill the other, do you really believe that will bring you happiness?'

As one, both Hook and Peter shouted out, 'Yes!'

Wendy was beyond frustration. She pleaded, 'You don't need this anymore, Peter. Stay in London, Peter, stay with me . . .'

Hook tried to counteract the propaganda with his own. 'Is that what you want, Pan? To grow up? Wear these ridiculous clothes, go to school, behave, mind your manners, and end up working in a bank?'

'It's not like that, Hook. Don't listen to him, Peter . . .'

'Don't listen to her, Pan,' Hook spat back.

The poor boy was stuck between the two.

'And as for growing up, isn't it time that *you* grew up, Hook?' Wendy asked with heavy sarcasm. 'Chasing little boys through the forests. I wonder, who is the child here?'

Hook didn't respond to that comment, although it clearly annoyed him. 'Listen to me, Pan, you and I have a destiny, it's in Neverland. I know that, you know that.'

Wendy could see that this was futile. 'Oh, I give up. If you're going to behave like savages, go ahead, but I will not allow you to do it here. This is a civilised place. Take it somewhere else. Take your fight back to Neverland.'

Hook paced the stage, head bowed, his hook placed discreetly behind his back. He looked like a properly trained Shakespearean actor. He stopped bottom stage right and called over to Pan, 'I do believe the young lady is right. We can't do this here.' He looked up to face Wendy and gave a curt bow. Turning back to Peter, he asked, 'What do you say, Pan? Return to where we both belong? And where we can once and for all decide who is the undisputed king of Neverland?'

Pan stayed silent but gave a focused, determined nod.

'Are we agreed then?' Hook asked. 'Do I have your word, Pan?'

'Returning to Neverland to defeat you . . . oh, nothing would give me more pleasure. You have my word, old man.'

'Good form Pan, good form!' Hook was happy, Peter was happy. As for Tink, she was ecstatic, and enthusiastically clapping her tiny hands.

'Miss Bell? Where are you? I need your assistance.'

Tink flew down from her spot high on a theatre spotlight and landed on Hook's left shoulder.

'Fairy dust, if you'd be so kind . . .' said Hook with an air of superiority.

Tink looked at Peter, who gave her a nod to go ahead, before flying up and over Hook, sprinkling him with her magic dust as she did so.

'But remember, you'll still need a happy thought,' she reminded Hook.

'Don't you worry your pretty little head – I've got this happy thought thing all sorted out,' said Hook. 'My happy thought? Finally getting the chance to defeat Peter Pan and having Neverland all to myself.'

And with that, Hook rose three feet off the stage, and his physical body began to dissolve. It was breath-taking to watch and even Wendy, still in the dress circle, gasped. As Hook's physical form dissolved in front of their very eyes, he looked up and spoke directly to Mr Barrie, who had appeared back in the dress circle. For the last ten minutes, he'd been out front in the foyer, worried he'd come face to face with a startled audience as they left the theatre after that dramatic curtain closing. But nothing could have been further from the truth.

As he stood out front, anxious, everyone had congratulated him. He was slapped on the back and had his hand shaken so many times and with such vigour that it hurt. The praise flowed from the audience, '*Congratulations Mr Barrie . . . What a play . . . What an ending . . . Didn't see that one coming . . . spectacular flying scene . . . how did you do it . . . I didn't even spot the wires . . . where the devil did you find that actor who played Hook, he was marvellous!*'

Barrie, although lost for words, had no choice but to accept the praise. So he did, but with a feeling of unease. What was he supposed to tell them? That it was all true? That Captain Hook and Peter Pan were real live people? He'd be a laughing stock, and his reputation ruined.

Once everyone had gone, Barrie breathed an immense sigh of relief. Yet he knew the hard part was yet to come – he still had to explain to the cast, the crew and the theatre management what really had just happened in there.

As he entered the dress circle, Barrie took in the sight of Hook, suspended in mid-air and starting to disintegrate. It was pure magic, the like of which even his writer's imagination could never have conjured up. Suddenly, Hook spotted him and called out.

'Now I remember you! Well, a word of warning, Mr Barrie. No more lies about Hook. Write about me, yes, but tell your audiences of Hook the hero, Hook the brave, Hook the greatest pirate who ever lived! Or I may come back to pay you a visit one day.' And with that last remark, and a wicked smile on his face, he slowly dragged his hook across his throat in a chilling warning.

Seconds later, Hook dissolved into a million tiny glittering lights, and finally vanished. The last thing to be heard, even after he could no longer be seen, was 'See you in Neverland, Pan!'

* * *

With Hook gone, Peter flew up and landed on the edge of the dress circle railing. 'Hello, Mr Barrie.'

'Hello Peter . . .' Barrie tentatively shook Pan's hand.

Peter flashed a huge grin at him. 'I enjoyed your play, Mr Barrie. Will you write more stories? Stories about me and my adventures?'

'I . . . I . . . why, yes, I, eh, I suppose that's possible,' stammered the author.

'Great! You must also mention the mermaids and pirates and witches. Listen to Wendy, she'll tell you everything you need to know, then just use your imagination. I think that won't be a problem for you. You believe in me and Neverland, don't you Mr Barrie?'

'Oh yes, I do. I truly do. And I'll let you into a secret: despite being the middle-aged man you see before you, I too have never really grown up.'

They smiled at each other, before Mr Barrie quietly

backed away, to give Peter and Wendy the space they obviously needed.

'I'll be over here, Wendy, if you need me.'

Sitting on the edge of the balcony rail, Peter faced Wendy. He was glowing, and had that old spark in his eyes. A spark long gone, a spark she had not seen since they were together in Neverland. He was alive again, and she realised that however much she wanted him to stay in London, and for them to grow up together, in her heart of hearts, she knew she could not keep him.

'I love you, Peter,' she said with total honesty.

While there was still a young boy's wish inside Peter to laugh off the comment, get embarrassed or make fun of it by pulling a face, he knew this was not the time. Although Peter Pan was never going to grow up properly, he had definitely done some growing up these past few months. He leaned in close and took Wendy's hands in his. Tink, perched close by on a spotlight, didn't like the look of where this was going.

'I love you too, Wendy,' replied Peter with as much grown-upness as he could muster.

Tink scrunched up her face, then made an over-the-top gesture of pushing two fingers down her throat and pretending to be sick.

'Come with me, Wendy, come back to Neverland! Just think of the adventures we'd have together! I'll build you a house and . . .'

Peter continued talking but his voice faded away, as Wendy thought about her life. Then she interrupted him. 'Stop, Peter, stop. I accept I can't make you stay in London, and frankly it was wrong of me to even try. But I can't go back to Neverland with you. No matter how much part of me wants that. You believe me when I say that, don't you, Peter?'

He nodded, resigned to what she was going to say.

'I'm staying in London, Peter. It's time for me to grow up.'

Peter nodded sadly, while Tink, mightily relieved, puffed out her tiny cheeks and gave a sigh of relief.

'I understand, Wendy. But don't worry, I'll fly back to London to visit you and—'

'No, Peter. Please don't.'

He put on his sulky face as Wendy continued. 'Peter, it would be too hard for me. Remember, I'm going to grow up, and I'll even have my own family someday. It just wouldn't be fair, on either of us . . .'

This time, Peter didn't argue.

'OK, Wendy. But never forget me, and remember I'll always be there for you, in that magical space, between being asleep and awake . . .'

Wendy smiled. This was painful, yet such beautiful words. Tink, still acting the fool, was now playing an imaginary violin.

'Tink!' scolded Peter.

She knew she was in the wrong and offered a humble, 'Sorry Peter, sorry Wendy.'

Wendy turned back to Pan, more seriously now.

'Peter, are you not scared to return to Neverland now that Hook is back and more dangerous than ever? He wants to kill you. This is not a game, Peter.'

Peter had now totally transformed back into his childlike self as he replied, 'But it *is* a game, the best game.'

'It's not, Peter. It's not a game. Hook will kill you.'

Peter's eyes sparkled. 'No, he won't, Wendy. I'm Peter Pan, remember? But if he did somehow, against the odds, succeed . . . well, all I can say is that to die would be an awfully big adventure!' He squealed as he propelled himself backwards into the air.

Wendy laughed, smiled and shook her head at the same time as tears of sadness and joy cascaded down her face.

Now hovering in mid-air, just beyond the rim of the dress circle, Peter blew Wendy a last kiss, before turning to Tink and announcing with pride, 'C'mon Tink, let's go! Second star on the right and straight on 'til morning!'

As Peter and Tink disappeared in a whirl of light, Wendy stood up, full of so many mixed emotions, and in what was barely a whisper, to an empty theatre, said with all the passion she could muster, 'I love you, Peter Pan and always will. Stay the way you are, my special boy. Never grow up, Peter Pan. Never ever ever grow up . . .'

CHAPTER 28

In need of a handkerchief, Wendy reached into her small purse, which was still hanging round her neck. As she fumbled within it, her hand brushed against something solid. What was this? She was sure it didn't belong to her.

Wendy took out the object. A miniature glass bottle, with a cork stopper at the end.

She looked at Mr Barrie with puzzlement written on her face. On closer examination, she realised it was a bottle of Tink's fairy dust.

'Peter must have dropped it in there earlier. Wait, there's tiny writing on the label.'

'What does it say?' asked an intrigued Mr Barrie.

'It says . . . sprinkle, believe and fly . . .'

With confused longing on her face, Wendy looked at Mr Barrie, at the bottle in her hands, then back up to Mr Barrie again. She was tormented by her decision, yet at the same time resigned.

Mr Barrie said as gently as he could, 'Sometimes you have to let go of the people you love most, in order not to crush their dreams. And we each must look into our hearts, for only there will we find the answer to where our future lies.'

Mr Barrie let those words sink in before continuing, 'Come, Wendy, I'll walk you home.'

CHAPTER 29

Wendy left the theatre with Mr Barrie, and was grateful for his company. He was a genuine friend and a true gentleman. But, wanting time on her own to try and make sense of what had just happened, Wendy walked the last half-hour of her journey alone, lost in her own thoughts.

It was all so surreal. Was it only a year ago that Peter Pan had miraculously arrived at her bedroom window? And the adventure to Neverland – pure magic, all of it.

She never once regretted her decision to take her brothers and fly home. But then Peter had returned, and although they'd shared wonderful times together once he'd decided to stay in London, she now wished he'd never come back. For the first time in her young life, Wendy was beginning to understand the pain of separation.

She was shattered and emotionally drained. She had no tears left, yet she still rubbed at her moist eyes and nose, now cold from the winter chill. She truly loved Peter.

But what did she love? The boy, the myth, or the man she'd hoped he'd one day become, but in reality now never would?

She knew in her heart of hearts that Peter could never have stayed in London. But had she made the wrong decision in not returning to Neverland? What was so special about growing up, after all?

Enough.

Her brain couldn't take any more analysing. She longed for bed and sleep. For a week. A month. A year. Forever.

It was nearly eleven by the time Wendy opened the gate and trudged up the path to the Darling family front door. It was freezing, with a crunchy frost underfoot. She pulled her jacket tight around her now shivering body.

As she got to the front door, she turned around and looked up at the night sky. A black sky with no clouds. Yet strangely, no stars. Odd.

Suddenly and out of nowhere, the brightest shooting star she'd ever seen appeared directly above her. Wendy couldn't take her eyes off it. But it didn't shoot off, it paused high in the sky, hovering directly above her.

Totally focused on the star, Wendy remembered Mr Barrie's words about letting go. Yet she also recalled these words, 'We each must look into our hearts, for only there will we find the answer to where our future lies.'

Wendy slipped her chilly hands into her jacket pocket while still marvelling at the solo star, hanging in the sky, gently pulsing with light.

Her hand brushed against the bottle of fairy dust. She took it out, held it up to the light of the star and read the label quietly to her herself.

'Sprinkle, believe and fly . . .'

THE END

OR IS IT?

Many years have passed since they last parted company in that London theatre, and life has not exactly been kind to Wendy. Now aged twenty-five, she is back living at home caring for her elderly father.

In Neverland, where time moves in a mysterious way or even seems to stand still . . . everyone is still exactly the same age. Peter Pan is still the boy who almost, but never grew up . . .

The Opacanta and the Lost Boys fight the witches, while the mermaids are in battle with the pirates who have turned the *Jolly Roger* into a whaling ship.

All rather normal for Neverland really.

However, their special world is soon shattered. As with Australia and America before, Neverland is 'discovered' by the outside world.

Gold diggers and loggers arrive and begin to ravage the pristine environment. The white man also brings disease that threatens to wipe out the Opacanta.

Has the time finally come for Neverland's various groups to stop fighting each other and work together to save their unique habitat?

But can they do it? Can Hook and Pan really join forces, especially after so much bloodshed on each side?

Back in London, in the Darling family attic, a depressed Wendy finds an old, long-forgotten bottle. On blowing off the dust, she studies the label.

It reads, 'sprinkle, believe and fly.'

Can an adult Wendy return to Neverland? And what will

a still young Peter Pan make of his childhood sweetheart, now a grown woman?

Hold onto your hats, it's about to get *a lot darker*.

The Battle for Neverland

Coming in Spring 2023 . . .

I wish to thank the following people

Louise Dickie for her advice on the concept of the book.

My editor Sam Boyce for making this book so much better than it initially was.

Angelina Antiukova for the cover design, website, and a whole heap of other stuff I'm not capable of doing.

DC Thomson publishers for their support in promoting this book.

Great Ormond Street Hospital for their invaluable advice and feedback.

And of course, J. M. Barrie, for without his talent, this book would have never been written. Thank you. You, sir, are a genius.

ABOUT THE AUTHOR

Born in Aberdeen, George R. Mitchell is a Scottish newspaper columnist of many years. He has travelled extensively in over eighty countries, writing predominantly on the topics of politics, religion and cultural division.

However, with a lifelong passion for original classic stories, especially Peter Pan, he decided with thanks to lockdowns, to finally write *An Awfully Big Adventure*.

It is aimed not just at children from middle grade and up, but young-at-heart adults who are looking for escapism and nostalgia.

This book is the first in a trilogy of new Peter Pan stories . . .

For more information visit us at wanallah.com

Printed in Great Britain
by Amazon

87062012R10130